Candy and Creeps

A WITCHY CANDY SHOP MYSTERY, BOOK 2

NYX HALLIWELL

Beach
Path
Publishing
LLC

Candy and Creeps, A Witchy Candy Shop Mystery, Book 2

©2024 Nyx Halliwell

ISBN: 978-1-964028-03-3

A house of illusions,
a cloak of disguise,
a web of enchantments,
woven with lies.
To break the spell,
to shatter the night,
the candy witch must follow whispers of starlight.
As her prophecy unfolds in a frightful embrace,
the faery tale princess bound by grace,
shall unearth the secrets in the light's revealing glow,
and Ever After's magic once more shall grow.

Chapter One

"Ever notice how there are no vampyres in faerytales?" I muse out loud.

The chubby strawberries lined up on wax paper in neat rows on my work table don't reply. A few test pieces have been dipped in white chocolate to resemble Santa's beard, and I've drawn eyes and mouths on them with dark chocolate piping.

The strawberry Santas stare at me with rapt attention. Yes, I'm talking to fruit. On this early winter morning inside my candy shop, there is no one else to listen.

"Faerytales aren't real," a male voice says from the shadowy corner. "Vampyres are."

I stop in mid-dip, the white chocolate—the same shade as my hair—drips off the strawberry's point. "What are *you* doing here?"

No point in adding *and how did you get in*? Simple locks do not stop Torren and his kind, a fact I've learned in the past eight weeks since arriving in Enchanted Haven.

Master vampyres, like the enticing one across from me, aren't even stopped by my strongest wards.

His only reply is a smile. A smile that sends a shiver of anticipation through me.

Onyx, my gargoyle protector in the form of a pendant, remains cool, and while I know Torren would never hurt me, my mind cautions me to be careful. Vampyres are always after something, even him.

Not only does he make my pulse speed up, but he smells of warm cognac and caramel. A combo I find impossible to resist. "It must be important for you to show up in person." Since my arrival, he and I have had a rather tumultuous relationship. He's determined to discover my secret origins and make me his queen. No one can know where I'm from under a decree by my mother, the queen of Ever After, and I have no desire for a throne. "Let me guess—you had a craving for my chocolate raspberry truffles."

His obsidian eyes flash a hint of gold as he steps into the light. "My craving cannot be satisfied by that kind of sweet."

Since Halloween, we've done this dance. He's tasted my royal blood, and his hunger for more has become unquenchable. He wants me to say yes to his proposal. I can't.

I shift back ever so slightly, trying not to sniff.

As stubborn as ogres in Ever After, he won't take no for an answer. To be honest, I'm not sure anyone has ever told him so. He's used to people obeying his every command, and he's made it his mission to woo, seduce, and conquer me.

No one, not even one as powerful and seductive as he is, will ever do so. I come from royalty but will never wear a crown. I'm *Outcast* from my beautiful faerytale kingdom, regardless that I'm the crown princess. Why? They claim I killed my best friend.

There's more to the story, and my memories have been tinkered with. A prophecy has alerted me that what happened

2

between me and Izzy is tangled up with magic and deception, and I'm going to use all my resources to unravel the truth and prove my innocence.

Willing myself not to show my attraction or anticipation, I re-dip the fruit and ignore the heat spreading south of my apron ties. It's always like this—I'm attracted to Torren more than I care to admit.

"Sugar is *always* the answer," I say, considering the idea that the cute Santas, staring at me mutely, might end up in my stomach. Sugar *is* always the answer for me. If I'm stressed, chocolate calms me. Sad? Cotton candy lifts my spirits. Happy? Any and all sweets will do.

As he steps closer, a predatory gleam in his eyes, I wish for a shield. Nothing is close, except a cake served and the bowl of melted white chocolate.

He picks up one of the fruits and toys with it, and I swear I hear high-pitched screams from all of them. "Your talent is wasted."

In Torren's world, that's code for: *come work for me.* And that happens to be code for: *Be my queen.*

"I'm the best baker in the area."

He takes another step. "Your scent is delicious. Irresistible."

Stepping away from him, I set the new Santa on the wax paper and warn my lower anatomy to stop purring at the compliment. I grip both sides of the bowl, prepared to dump the warm chocolate over his head if necessary. "Back off or suffer the consequences."

He's so close I notice the gold flecks in his dark eyes flashing, his pupils dilating. "A little nip to take the edge off? No harm will come to you, I swear it on my own grave."

Could anything stop him from being charming and irresistible? I should walk away, put space between us again. I don't. "Please. I know that works on humans, but how gullible do you think I am?"

One corner of his mouth quirks. He raises the strawberry to his nose. Inhaling deeply, he grins. "Not gullible. Strategic."

"This is not a game, and I'm attempting tact. I've already said no."

A finger reaches out as if he will stroke my cheek. I want him to, and yet, that would be bad. I pull back and he drops his hand. "The Guild meets in three days."

A vampyre get-together on Christmas Eve? I force my pulse to slow and avert my eyes. "How lovely for you. Have a good time."

He leans against the workbench. "I have intel that someone is planning an assassination, and I need your help."

Enchanted Haven is a unique town, and since it's been designated *neutrum*—neutral territory for all supernaturals— no faction has power over another. My candy shop is in the heart of Main Street, and I'm determined to work with the other business owners to do my part to keep things peaceful. The thought of someone being targeted makes my skin crawl. "Who would do such a thing? Who are they after?" I set the bowl down hard when a new thought strikes. "You?"

"If I were the target, I would welcome the challenge."

No doubt he would. It wouldn't be the first time that another vampyre has tried to eliminate him in order to take over the region. "Enchanted Haven has been declared neutral ground since we captured the kobolds." Nasty creatures with origins in Ever After were targeting innocent humans at Halloween. Torren and I, along with my godmother, Marlena, and the resident lycan shifter, Cyn, were able to stop their killing spree. "No supernatural would be stupid enough to break the pact that keeps it so."

4

"There is no honor among supernaturals." He juggles the fruit between his hands. "I must ask a favor to ensure the pact is enforced and the refuge of the town remains intact."

I glance around my tiny kitchen, wishing I could sink through the floor. I'm not one to run from a fight; on the other hand, I want no part of a supernatural war. I've only just become accepted here by the mundanes and magical alike. My godmother and I secretly help other Outcasts from our realm to navigate the ins and outs of humandom.

On my collarbone, Onyx heats, reflecting my anxiety—or possibly a genuine threat.

Torren scrutinizes my face, making sure I see the gravity of the situation reflected in his. "If a supernatural war erupts, humans will suffer."

I fiddle with one of the candies. The lure of the sugar rush is hard to resist.

"Witches will be enslaved," he continues, his voice so quiet that I catch myself leaning toward him. "You will be prized above all others—forced to do Cambria's bidding if she gains control."

My insides curl as my backbone straightens. "I will do no one's *bidding*." My powers are far beyond that of a mortal witch. "Who is this Cambria?"

"She is a hybrid. Part vampyre, part witch. Referred to as the Queen of the Cursed."

Interesting. I doubt she's more powerful than me, but I can't be sure. My magic doesn't work here the way it did in Ever After. "No one can enslave me, and faction wars aren't my business."

He returns to the other side of the table. The strawberry Santa he's juggled lands with a thunk on the wax paper. Juice bleeds from it.

"Be careful!" I grab a towel to wipe it up. "I have to make one hundred and forty-four of these things for the Christmas Open House tomorrow, along with dozens of cookies. Strawberries this time of year are hard to come by."

Muscles under his expensive suit bulge as he places his fists on either side of the cookie sheet. "I'll pay whatever cost necessary."

There's more to that statement than the price of fruit. I anticipate Christmas will be my best—and most profitable—holiday, next to Halloween. Since funds are scarce due to my cranky oven and walk-in fridge dying at the same time, I need those profits. Each appliance is decades out of date, and a fluke lightning strike recently zapped both.

At least, I think it was a fluke. The weather has been erratic lately, and it smells of magic.

"Name your price," he says. "Come with me to The Guild meeting, help me stop this assassin, and I'll repay you with anything you desire."

Creating a faery bargain with a prince of the night—a handsome one at that—is still out of the question. A bargain always has a price. Sure, he can deliver the hard-to-get fruits and provide me with new appliances, but then I'd owe him. "I don't know what you think I can do, but my answer is no. I won't be your date, your queen, or your partner in any of this."

His impossible-to-miss bulges twitch under the fabric, fists flexing. "If the target were anyone else, I would handle it alone. As it is, I am too close to the situation to think clearly. I need someone with perspective and your...skillset."

I bite my lip, trying not to stare at his muscular arms. Arms that once carried and held me as if I were a delicate and rare jewel. Is it wrong that I long to feel them around me again? If he knew the extent of my skills, he might fear me. He's only seen the surface level of my magic.

For him to admit he's not thinking clearly surprises me, and I focus on that. He never reveals weakness—I didn't know it was possible. He's the epitome of detached and logical. Who or what would cause him to act emotional? Dare I say, *human*?

"Are you in love?"

"What?"

"Why don't you ask her to be your queen?"

He straightens, exasperated. "There is no one I'm interested in besides you."

Back to that. "It's my blood, nothing more."

He gives a feral smile. "It is much, much more."

The dangerous energy pouring off him reminds me he is a predator. One who has been after me since my arrival here.

Instinctively, I step back, reaching for a cake server. "Torren, seriously. I can't help you. You have to leave. I have a business to run."

He doesn't miss the sharp edge of the blade as the metal glints in my nervous grip. His features morph from haughty and predatory to something else—worry. "Seraphina, on my honor, I'll give you anything you want if you do this for me. Stop the assassin, and I'll protect you for the rest of your life. You'll never have to worry about a thing."

The handle is cool in my sweaty palm. What would make a master vampyre offer to be under my thumb? Since he doesn't even know the full extent of my powers, or the constant reason I need to be careful and keep them hidden, he indeed must fear this assassin.

Or perhaps I *am* gullible. Maybe he knows all about me and is using this ploy to get me to agree to his proposal. Marlena is always warning me not to trust his kind; I must be careful. "Who's the target?" I'm sure I won't like the answer, but he doesn't give it to me.

So annoying.

He heads for the exit instead. "I've frightened you, and that was not my intent."

"Wait." I follow, Onyx nearly blistering my skin. I tug on his arm. "Tell me who Cambria is after."

He stops and peers at me, seemingly ready to spill the jelly beans. Before he can, however, a linebacker-sized male dressed in all black blocks the exit. "I thought I smelled a dead man," Cyneric, the lycan shifter, growls at Torren.

From the look in his eyes, the town reverend is ready to start his own war.

And it's over me.

Gulp.

Chapter Two

"You need to upgrade your wardrobe." Torren brushes a hand over the shoulder of Cyn's jacket as if dislodging a hair. "And perhaps some new shower gel. It's hard to smell anything over the scent of wet dog."

Cyn lives at the church next door. He and the vampyre are friends, yet you wouldn't know it at times. Cyn says it's a male thing—the constant harassment and competitiveness. Under it all, Cyn thinks the world of Torren, and vice versa.

Still, Cyn is overly protective of me, demonstrating his alpha instincts. He must have sensed my unease over Torren's presence, even from across the way.

He isn't in a joking mood tonight, his dark brown peepers scanning Torren's face. "State your business, and it better not include badgering my favorite baker."

Torren glances my way. "She is my favorite, too." The tone of his voice softens. "I give my word, Seraphina. You will be well compensated if you accept my offer."

He vanishes into the darkness of my small backyard.

"He just won't let it go, will he?" Cyn advances to the

table. He thinks this is all about Torren's goal of making me his queen.

"You don't need to worry." I wipe my hands on a fresh towel and motion at his attire. "Give me your jacket."

"Why?"

I grab the lapel and tug. "Catnip dust."

"Huh?"

He looks at the shoulder where Torren left a sprinkling of it. The shifter can't see it, but I can. "Don't sniff."

His nose wrinkles, natural instinct warring with my command. He shrugs off the jacket, and I whisk it away, dumping it in my sink of dishwater to soak.

"I'm not a cat. Why did he do that?"

"Pettiness probably. Regardless of your nature, it would knock you out for a while, but do you no lasting harm." It might also give someone like me the ability to track Cyn. But a vampyre? He shouldn't be able to use it that way. It makes me wonder what he's doing with it.

"The important question is where he got it." I smack Cyn's hand when he reaches for a strawberry. "Do not touch those. I have to deliver one hundred and forty-four of them to The Chamber come sunrise, and I'm already running out."

"Sorry." He gives me puppy dog eyes—literally. "Also, that I didn't get here sooner. I had a parishioner in need of counseling."

I pat his hand. "I appreciate your concern, but I don't need a bodyguard. We've talked about this—your territorial predilection."

His large shoulders slump. "I know. I can't help it. I'm an alpha—it's what I do."

I could use magic to reheat the hardened white chocolate, but it's important to use my ability sparingly so I don't overtax myself. The laws and dynamics here drain me faster than in Ever After, so I use the microwave instead. "Torren claims there's an assassin going after a vampyre at the upcoming Guild meeting. Some hybrid—Cambria?—is behind it."

"The Guild meets here specifically because it's neutral ground. When the heads of the supernatural communities are all in one place, they're sitting ducks. This way, they're off-limits and untouchable during the meeting. If anyone, even her, violates the Treaty..." He gives a visible shudder. "The consequences are extreme."

I don't want to know what those are. The microwave dings. I stir the chocolate and resume dunking the fruit. "What can you tell me about her?"

His shirt stretches across his chest when he sets his hands on his hips. While I haven't seen him preach, I imagine he does this when he's about to begin a sermon. "Other than she's a greedy, power-hungry monster who wants everyone under her thumb?"

I wonder again who she's targeting—competition from the sounds of it. "Getting the Undead Nation under her control would give her almost unstoppable power. That would definitely be a problem for all of us."

"She's wicked, there's no question about it, but she's not strong enough to take over Torren's nest." His eyes darken to the color of chocolate. "Is she?"

Cyn realizes I'm not a 'normal' witch yet assumes I have some kind of connection to the witchy hotline. "Would taking out a high-level master like Torren weaken the Undead enough for her to overcome them with force?"

He considers it, eyeing a tray of day-old cookies. One finger points to them, and he lifts a brow in question.

I nod, and he grabs the largest one. The shifter is always

hungry. "Some of the hybrids might follow her, but not the true vamps," he says around a mouthful. "These are excellent."

He's easy to please. "Then why is Torren offering me everything, including an Undead throne, to stop this assassin? Who do think is the target?"

We stare at each other for a moment, both of us considering possibilities. I see a spark in Cyn's eyes. "Oh, dog bones."

His version of swearing. "What?" I ask.

A shake of his head sends his hair cascading over his shoulders. "It's a myth. It can't be true."

Anything can be true. "Tell me."

Propping himself against the counter, he inhales a second cookie, his gaze pinned on the rows of Santas. "My clan's elders used to speak about an ancient supernatural that the vampyres claim relation to. He's prophesized to rise from the grave someday and allow the Undead to rule the world. He has necromantic abilities and can shift into a variety of forms. Worse, he can also procreate. You know, raise the dead and make babies at the same time. He would command magic like we've never seen."

Bitter butterscotch, that's frightening.

He swallows a mouthful. "If such a creature exists, Cambria would certainly want to kill it."

"Because it would be a threat to her?"

"Absolutely."

"Is there a name for the creature?"

His nose scrunches. "Nightbane. There are a lot of theories about when and where he'll rise, but they're only guesses. Like I said, Nightbane is a myth."

Most assume faerytales are make-believe. I know better. "Something's got Cambria willing to break the sanctuary convenient to destroy it. Do you think Nightbane may rise here?"

He dismisses the idea with a wave. "Nah, like I said, it's not real."

I make work of lining up the newest candies to draw on their faces. Using a pastry bag of warmed chocolate, I create two eyes and a round mouth on the first. "Hypothetically, if Nightbane *was* real and here, wouldn't Cambria try to harness his power rather than kill him?"

"He's too powerful to control. He's the ultimate Undead with a side of shapeshifter and who knows what else?"

So he's god-like. "What did the prophecy predict he'd do if he does rise?"

His shoulders slump, and he sets down the uneaten portion of the cookie. "It's bye-bye to life as we know it."

"He'll be able to control all of us?"

"That's what world domination typically involves." He says this with a bit of a *duh* in his voice, as if I'm dimwitted.

"Domination of humans, as well as supernaturals?"

The *duh* tone takes over his features this time. "Of course."

"To kill them?"

He boosts off the table. "Seven billion humans live on this planet. Some will be pressed into servitude; others will be breakfast, lunch, and dinner for Nightbane and his followers. Smart money would be to keep a percentage of them alive and reproducing so there's always a fresh supply of food."

Gumdrops, my stomach is turning over on itself. "Blood slaves." I set down the pastry bag, the implications overwhelming. "If Cambria wants to destroy Nightbane, I think I'm in favor of her doing so."

"She's not exactly the lesser of two evils, and Nightbane is fiction." He peers into the dishwater. "That's my best jacket. Is it salvageable?"

"I'll let you know after I've cleaned it." Which involves magic. "But probably."

"Thanks, and don't worry." He kisses my forehead, a brotherly gesture. The gargoyle doesn't heat—Cyn is safe. "Torren will handle whatever is going on. Stay out of it."

"Ease up on the alpha orders, okay?"

He gives an apologetic smile. "Do you want me to stay in case he returns?"

I'm never truly alone, but I appreciate his offer. It's been weeks since Torren paid me a visit, and I've been lax on reinforcing my wards—not so much because I worry about the vampyre, but the ghosts? Since landing here, I've gained the ability to see and hear them, and they drive me bonkers. "Marlena will be back in no time, and I've got plenty of work to do. I'll freshen my wards."

He squeezes my arm and nods. "I'm just across the way," he reminds me. "Your personal bodyguard anytime you need me."

I smile as he leaves, but it looks like I'm the one who needs to protect him.

The vampyre is right. Lady Wyndolynn, my cat familiar, licks her paw under the table. I didn't even notice her sneaking in. *The wolf stinks.*

"He's a good person," I retort. "Why don't you make yourself useful and—"

Sir Nibbles, our resident mouse, squeaks from the arch of his home in the wall, taunting the cat. Instantly, she's on her feet, hissing. Before I can stop her, she streaks across the tile and slams into the plaster, one white-tipped paw diving inside the hole.

"You fall for that every time," I tease. Sir Nibbles is as bad as Cyn and Torren, always trying to rile her up.

She continues to paw at him, trying to snag his tiny body. *Mind your own business.*

Marlena rushes in, bringing a gust of cool night air with her. "We've got trouble."

"Yes, I heard about Cambria and the assassin."

"Who?"

Oops, she's talking about something else, most likely the Outcast family she's helping. "What is it? Are the children okay?"

"They're fine. Well, as fine as they can be after losing their home this time of year. It's not that—I felt a troublesome ripple in the magic here." She removes her coat and hangs it on a hook near the door. Her short curls bob with anxiety. The higher her stress level, the tighter they curl. "Something dark and dangerous is coming."

Nightbane. "Can you be more specific?"

Her eyes grow the size of giant lollipops. "Whatever it is, it's evil."

My stomach flips. Even the strawberries hold no appeal. "Help me finish these."

"Seraphina, I'm serious. We may need to flee and help the others do so. It would be prudent to plan for an evacuation."

"And go where?" I know how to fight monsters in Ever After. The ones of this world can't be all that different. Besides, I refuse to run at the first sign of trouble. "This is our home now. I'm not leaving."

Her hand instinctively goes to her waist, but her sword isn't there. Gunther is upstairs in his sheath—she hasn't needed him since Halloween. "Princess, whatever this is, it's not going to be managed with a few of your candies. Our lives may be in peril. This magic is...dangerous."

The cat, having lost interest in her prey, strolls past. *She's right.*

"*I'm* dangerous," I remind her. "For now, we act normal." I continue working on the Santas, their open mouths mocking me. "We are not without resources, and no one is chasing us from our home."

She washes her hands and dons a matching apron with our shop's name on it—The Candy Cauldron. "I hope you know what you're doing."

So do I, I think, and pop a Santa to calm my nerves.

Chapter Three

"This year's Give A Gift night is going to be bigger and better than ever!" Betty Marple, the mayor's assistant, claps her hands and rubs them together as she eyes the treats I've brought for the open house.

"Yes, Betty," I say, handing over the Santas. "You've done a fantastic job putting it together."

Her green dress is a size too small, the fabric of the costume stretched to the point of bursting over her generous curves. Her jaws jiggle as she hustles me to the town hall's conference room, laid out with tables and chairs. "They don't call us Enchanted Haven for nothing."

Her elf hat rests on one end of a folding table covered with a vinyl red cloth. The centerpiece is a house decorated with Christmas lights and miniature pine trees.

"Are you getting plenty of business?" she asks, eyeing the rows of strawberries in the first container. "When I went by yesterday morning, there was a line out your door."

I can see in her intense focus that she's looking for the plumpest one to snag for herself. "Yes, plenty."

Once the Santas are set out to her standards, I hand her a tiered container full of decorated cookies and check my watch. "Can you take care of these? I have to get back and open up."

"I thought you might stay for a cup of coffee, Ms. Fairchild," a male voice says from the doorway.

"Good morning, Mayor. I wish I could."

He leans on the door frame, thumbs hooked in his belt loops. His magic fills the room and tickles mine. I force myself not to giggle and give away the fact I can sense it. "You didn't happen to bring me one of your angel food cakes, did you?"

I remove a white paper bag from my tote. "How could I forget?"

His lazy grin stretches across his face. He boosts off the frame, meeting me in the middle of the room, as Betty chats on and on about the day's itinerary. He lowers his voice while accepting the bag. "Heard you had an unwelcome visitor last night."

The air glitters with his angel magic. "Cyn filled you in?"

A quick dip of his chin as he calls out a random comment to Betty, who's now fussing with napkins, laying piles of them out amongst the serving trays. Her sister is a human witch but she's nonmagical—mundane. "I know Torren's your friend, but have a care with him. With the holiday and The Guild meeting, things around here will be... fraught with potential calamity."

"I'm aware, but Torren won't hurt me."

"His lot is unpredictable. You know I think highly of him, just like you do, but The Guild puts enormous pressure on him. He could snap. I'm considering placing our town under a few protective wards."

If Mayor Jo does that, he'll keep out *all* supernaturals. That could very well ruin the festivities. From what Betty says, the town counts on this huge bash every year—we can't afford not to have it.

I can't afford not to have it.

Besides, I need to figure out if this prophecy about Nightbane is true, because if it is, that's worse than Torren bugging me. "I can handle him," I murmur as Betty hustles to us, hat on. "And he can The Guild."

"The candy and cookies are perfect!" She claps her hands again, the fabric around her upper arms straining. "Thank you so much, Seraphina."

I'm embraced in a cloud of Aqua Net and Chanel Number Five. Her bear hug forces the air from my lungs.

Mayor Jo raises the white bag and steps away. "Appreciate this, Ms. Fairchild. Tell your godmother I said hello."

He and Marlena have been dancing around each other since we arrived in town. I nod, and he leaves, then Betty follows me to the door. "You're coming to the tree lighting tonight, right?"

"I'm afraid I'll miss it. Marlena and I will be serving hot cocoa and handing out peppermint lollypops at the store for the shoppers."

"Oh, but you have to close for a few minutes and attend! It's tradition!"

Most of the year, the town is adorned for Halloween, but this festival is given equal weight. Since it's my first holiday season here, I need to learn their expectations of me.

Betty, Mayor Jo, and most of the other shop owners have been supportive and inclusive—it's only right for me to be courteous and accommodating. "I'll see what I can do."

"Will you bring a date?" She waggles her brows at me. "I hear you're sweet on Torren, and tonight is magical. Very romantic." She winks.

The gossip mill here is fast, efficient, and filled with ladies like her who love the Aqua Net-and-perfume cocktail. "We're only friends, Betty."

Her sly look tells me she doesn't believe it. "Sure, you are. I wish *my* male friends looked at me the way he does you."

This gives me pause. "How exactly does he look at me?"

"Like you're the center of his world." She heaves a dreamy sigh. "As if he would move mountains for you."

If only I knew if that was because he actually cared for me, or because he only fancies my blood and seeks my agreement to become his queen. "I'm sure you're exaggerating."

"If you can't see it, you're blind." From behind her back, she draws out a strawberry Santa and gives me a sorry expression. "I couldn't resist."

In Ever After, we celebrate a similar holiday with gift-giving and decorations, but here, they've raised the bar to monumental heights. Every doorway, window, and interior is trimmed with garland, bright ornaments, and white lights. Each yard is brimming with embellishments.

The dentist, Maude Trumble, who is certain I'm ruining the teeth of everyone, has fake snow on her tiny lawn—it never seems to get quite cold enough this far south for the real stuff —and has painted the corners of her windows to resemble frost. An inflated snowman rocks back and forth day and night, illuminated by a spotlight at night.

I've been surprised at the polarity the season causes in supernaturals and mundanes alike—they crave it and can't wait for it, yet it often leaves them sad and hollow. "What exactly does the tree lighting entail?"

Her eyes twinkle. "First, we draw for the person who gets to push the lever to light things up. We call them 'starlighters.' It's an honor to be chosen. Then the mayor says a few words, thanks the Chamber—namely, me—for all our hard work, and when he finishes, we count down from ten to one. The starlighter pushes the lever, and—" With her empty hand, she makes a bursting motion. "The tree lights the night! Afterward, carolers roam the sidewalks, and folks stroll Main Street to shop. They stop here to socialize and warm up."

"Sounds lovely." I force a smile as she bites into the candied fruit. It truly does, and I feel a rush of anticipation. This town is special, and I plan to enjoy it. I just hope it's not my first and last Christmas season here. "I'll see what I can do."

Chapter Four

On my way to the shop, I sense the pixies before I see them.

The tiny hairs on the back of my neck stand at attention and faerytale magic pricks my skin. In the morning rays of sunshine, I feel cold to the bone. I pick up my pace to near running.

Not here, I think, as locals pass me on the sidewalk calling greetings. Absentmindedly, I reply, hurrying past Alchemy Elixirs & Remedies, with its antique sign over the door offering potions and remedies to soothe the soul. The cool air turns frigid around me and I hug myself. The faintest dusting of snow scatters across the path in my wake.

Not snow—faery dust.

The glittering pixie energy flashes and darts about, mixing with the snowflake-shaped dust. Evergreens in planters festooned with red bows and trailing ivy tremble. The various shop entrances up and down the street, decorated with wreaths and garland, give the fast-moving Ever After beings plenty of hiding spots as they wait for me. Their presence heralds an incoming message.

"Good morning, Seraphina," Cyn calls from the open doors of the church. He's sweeping frost-tipped leaves from the stairs. "Did you get the treats delivered?"

I wave and reply through gritted teeth. "Yes. It took a few trips, but Betty has everything."

The sparkling lights slow their flitting, coalescing in front of me. The pressure in my ears builds.

Almost there. Almost...

Just as I reach my pretty display in front of The Candy Cauldron, my body goes rigid. The flashes of pixie energy, with their rainbow colors, become a solid bubble—a portal to the Ever After throne room.

"Gingersnap," I say under my breath.

The physical world around me fades, and the sound of royal trumpets blares in my ears. Onyx comes to life, scratching at the skin under my sweater.

I can't run anymore as the hologram takes shape in the air before me. The Queen's stern gaze is not softened by the gauzy, sparkling dress she wears, nor the fur stole that looks like pure *minchon*—a rare, expensive animal raised for their lustrous coat that grows ten inches a day. They must be shaved continuously and the fur shines with a luster none can match.

Her hair is coiled on top of her head, and a crown of butterflies flits about it. As if she were standing right in front of me, my mother's voice rings in my ears. "Help the vampyre thwart the assassin."

The command causes my backbone to vibrate as if someone has rung a bell inside me. My royal blood flows sticky and hot. There is no, *Hi, sweetie, how are you*? Or, *I hear you're doing great in the human world*.

Of course, I'm here because of her. She's the one who

spoke the decree to banish me. The entire kingdom thinks I killed Izzy, so I can't blame her for it—at least not logically.

But she's my mother. The woman who is supposed to know me better than anyone else. The one person I had total confidence in, admired, fashioned myself after, and tried to make happy at all costs. How could she believe such a thing of me?

A bitter taste hits my tongue. I don't expect a welcome home invitation, yet it rips my heart to pieces all over again that she banished me. That she's right in front of me and can't even give me a smile.

Body paralyzed—familiar magic that she used on me frequently in my youth to stop my shenanigans—all I can do is speak. "Good to see you, Mother," I lie. "Sorry, but no. I won't help him. To do so would violate—"

Ice invades my throat and chest, freezing further comment. She doesn't deign to command me to shut up, she simply wills it, her expression as chilly as the wintery air.

If my face wasn't a younger version of hers, no one would realize we're related. She doesn't even comment about the fact that most of my coloring was stripped away when I was forced through the portal into this place, leaving my skin pale and my hair white as the fake snowfall.

She refuses to use my name or my official title, mimicking the fact I have purposefully ignored hers. "It's not a request, *daughter*." Is it progress that she recognizes me as her progeny once more? If the edge of anger riding on the term is any indication, that answer is a hard no. "You will do as you're told."

I breathe in frost, the pockets of air in my lungs turning to ice cubes. I'm a spectacle in view of the entirety of businesses on Main Street. No one can see her or her minions, but they can see me, frozen in place, appearing to talk to myself, my breath creating crystals in front of my face.

Most disturbing, however, is the fact that in all the time I have known the Queen, she has never paid attention to humandom's supernaturals. She certainly has never supported the children of the night or their mission for power and domination. She cares not what happens here and certainly has no love for those who inhabit this realm.

Does she?

"What angle are you playing?" I whisper.

The faintest tremble of her lips suggests she heard me. "You will partner with the vampyre, and in return, he will come to your aide when I command." Her voice sends a fresh wave of frigid goosebumps down my spine—a binding contract, her magic as effective through the portal as it is in person.

I have no choice. The words are forced from my tongue. "Yes, Your Majesty."

"Your vow," she orders, no longer my parent, but the royal leader of Ever After. The contract must be sealed with my words.

Tears fill my eyes—not from sadness, from anger. My willpower is fighting hers. I show no resistance outwardly, no matter how I struggle against it internally. The words grind out of me. "I...vow...under the decree of the faery bargain...that I will assist Torren to stop the assassin."

A snapping effect vibrates through my being. She might as well have asked for a blood oath, the magical contract now unbreakable. Satisfied, she looks down her perfect nose at me and offers a smile. Not the one I long for, but one of satisfaction.

Before I can read anything more into it, the pixie energy

swirls once more, and her hologram vanishes. With a soft *pop*, the portal closes, the bubble blinking out.

"Seraphina?" Cyn is striding toward me, his thick brows furrowed. His long legs cover the distance effortlessly. "Are you ill? You look even paler than normal."

I shiver, physically trying to shake off the shackles of the deal I have struck. Invisible to others, they nevertheless brand me with threads to my mother and to Torren, sneaking along my skin like the finest spider's silk.

"I'm...fine." My voice is rough. I force my frozen lips into an overdone smile. "Lack of sleep, I guess, from making the Santas."

He reaches out a supportive hand, but all I want to do is get inside The Candy Cauldron and pretend this never happened. The shop's window displays of holiday cakes and candies beckon to me, promising an ease to my anger and anxiety.

Comfort.

Safety.

A car passes, honking at us to get out of the street. A trio of pedestrians have paused on the sidewalk to gawk.

Maude emerges from the dentist's office in her white lab coat. "Has all that sugar finally caused a seizure?" she calls. "Should I call the doctor?"

Cyn waves all of them off. "Everything's fine. Go on, now."

A flush of embarrassment rises up my neck. My cheeks flame. I don't need less sugar, as Maude believes, I need more.

At least I'm no longer shivering.

Cyn starts to take my arm, but I'm already moving. Dodging him, I trip over my own feet, staggering across the few feet to the sidewalk in an awkward nutcracker-like stride.

I lose my balance and fall. The wooden gingerbread men in

their festive scarves who welcome visitors splinter under my weight. Through the glass door, I see Marlena look up from helping a customer, shock raising her brows.

Cyn rushes to me. "Seraphina!"

"This can't be happening," I mutter, blowing out a breath to send a strand of hair out of my eyes.

"What?" he asks, bending down.

I shake my head, legs sprawled, sweater torn, and my cute greeters destroyed. I'd assumed I'd enjoy a fresh start here in Enchanted Haven. Make new friends, run my candy shop, and spread happiness to the townsfolk.

Yet, murder, mayhem, and magic have followed me. "It's nothing," I say, gritting my teeth as I pluck a splinter out of my hand.

Lady Wynnie appears on the sidewalk, her feline mouth curling in a gleeful smile. *Nothing but a faery bargain with the most powerful queen to ever rule.*

Chapter Five

"Oh, for heaven's sake, what happened?" Marlena helps me to my feet.

"I'm fine, really." Ignoring the sting on my knees from hitting the sidewalk, I pretend my mother's appearance hasn't shaken me.

Real snow is falling now, coating the street and sidewalk. As I brush some from my hands, Cyn grips my arm to steady me. "You were up all night, weren't you?"

Gently, I remove myself from his hold, offering a bright smile to both of them. "I tripped over the curb, that's all."

They stare at me with heavy frowns. Marlena collects my tote, hanging it on her shoulder. Our conversation about the magical ripple she felt last night replays in her eyes. Her curls nearly stand straight up. "We worked on those Santas until two. Neither of us had much sleep."

"She's paler than normal," Cyn adds as if I'm not standing right there.

I wave them off. "I'm always this pale. You're seeing things."

He won't be deterred. "When you froze in the street, you looked almost ghost-like."

Flower, an earth-bound spirit who pops in when least expected, and generally least wanted, appears behind him, peeking over his shoulder. Her eyes are big behind her round glasses. "You're as white as the snow!"

Today's attire is in keeping with her usual hippie fashion— bell-bottom pants and a crocheted vest over an orange shirt with bell sleeves. Since she's dead, the weather doesn't affect her. I, on the other hand, am once more chilled to the bone.

"I need sugar," I claim. "And coffee."

Cyn pats my shoulder. "You gave me quite a scare. Is Maude right? Did you have a seizure or something?"

Thankfully, he means well. "No, it was only..." *My mother.* I really do need a hit of sugar. My tongue is about to get me into trouble.

Luckily, Mrs. Jarvis arrives, all smiles as she's missed the show and is wrapped up in her own world. "Seraphina," she gushes, "I need to order a dozen of your muffins for this week-end. My kids are coming home. All of them! With their families. Can you believe it? My kids and grandkids all here at the same time!"

"That's wonderful," I say, feeling the hollow pit in my stomach of someone who has no family now. Thank goodness I have my godmother.

Marlena turns on her charm and escorts her inside to write up the order. With Cyn's help, I finish collecting the remains of the display. "Thanks," I tell him, stacking the broken pieces of wood. "It looks like I'll have to haul out the skeletons from Halloween and put scarves on them. I better get to work."

He doesn't let me off the hook. "It was only what?"

"Hmm?"

"Come on, Seraphina. You locked up like you were scared for your life a minute ago, then you went stumbling toadstool over tombstone. What gives?"

My mother chose to exile me rather than kill me for my crime. There are conditions to this punishment, however. One of them is that I never speak of Ever After or the type of magic that runs in my veins. To do so would be fatal. "It was nothing. The sun hit me in the eyes, and I was blinded for a moment."

"Sure. That's plausible." He rolls his eyes.

"Cyn, really. That's all. I'm tired, and I have a lot to do today. I'm up here," Using a finger, I mimic the wheels of my brain turning. Or maybe it looks like I'm suggesting I'm crazy. "In my head. Brainstorming with myself."

His frown tells me he still doesn't believe me. "Brainstorm about what?"

Nothing like putting a girl on the spot. Glancing up and down the street for eavesdroppers, I decide distraction is in order. I motion him closer and lower my voice. He'll find out anyway, so best I put my spin on it so he doesn't freak out and cause problems. "I'm going to accept Torren's offer."

"*What?*" His voice booms in the entrance and echoes down the street. "You're going to marry him?"

"No, no." I shake my head and gesture for him to lower his voice. That's all I need—the local gossips starting a rumor about me getting married. "Not *that*. I'm going to help him immobilize the assassin."

He blinks. "Are you out of your mind?"

I absolutely am, but if the Queen is ordering me to work with the vampyres, there's something suspicious going on. I need to know what, and I can't break a faery bargain.

"Hear me out. We need to know what the vampyres are up to and if Nightbane is more than a myth. We also need a heads-up on what Cambria is planning and how she's going to do it. The best way to find all that out is for me to go undercover and investigate."

He crosses his arms and studies the treats in the display window as if an answer is hidden in them. "You're playing with fire."

Fire. My memory flashes with the past—Izzy and the flames in my oven. I shudder, suddenly dizzy. I drop the wooden pieces I've collected and put a hand on the window to steady myself.

"Seraphina!" He grabs both of my arms. "You are *not* all right, and I don't think this change of heart is wise."

There are few things that scare me, but the idea of any of the major players in this game—whether it be the vampyres, Cambria, or my mother—getting the upper hand is quite terrifying. I wish Izzy were here to give me guidance.

I refuse to freak out, though, until I know the facts. "If you have a better idea, I'm all ears. The only way I can see to get the answers we need and keep the world safe is if I'm on the inside. Then, we can control the outcome."

"Whatever that might be," Flower adds, nodding.

Princess Wynnie watches us with her green cat eyes. *You're braver than I thought.*

Cyn must realize what it would mean for shifters, including him. He releases his hold but continues to resist the idea. "I don't like it."

That makes two of us. "Do you have a better plan?"

His lips part with a heavy sigh. "To get on the inside of The Guild, you'll have to become Torren's queen."

The thought makes me want to run and hide, but I can't. I *won't.* I care about this realm and these beings, and I must uncover what my mother is up to. "I'll do what it takes to save us, but I doubt it will come to me agreeing to that. All I have to do is stop Nightbane and Cambria. Easy as divinity." *Not.*

"I've never made candy, so I'll take your word for it." His bushy brows are tight. "But tricking the Undead only ever ends in blood. Torren will be furious if—*when*—he discovers you've deceived him. One way or another, he'll bind you to him."

A fate worse than death. He can try, but it won't work. My heritage makes me pretty much indestructible, and although there is no precedence regarding vampyres and faery princesses being bound by blood, so far, he's the one following *me* around like a dog begging for a bone. I'm counting on the fact that I'm immune to him.

"We should get your jacket." I meet Cyn's gaze head-on, letting him know it's decided. He's not changing my mind. His return stare tells me he plans to try and do so regardless.

Our face-off is short-lived once I lift my chin and channel my mother's inner majesty. He uncrosses his arms and shakes his head. "Fine, but you're going to need a bodyguard for real."

I don't, but it's sweet that he thinks so. Seems like everyone in town believes I am as soft as my confections. They underestimate me, and I find it annoying, but it helps me keep a low profile. "I assume you're volunteering?"

He gives a half-hearted smile and opens the door for me, causing the bell to jingle. "Let's get you that coffee and sugar. Then we'll devise our plan."

Chapter Six

Marlena and I work nonstop all morning serving customers. Cyn stews and tries to pinpoint how he can protect me while I'm undercover.

I allow him to strategize in the small courtyard out back, Wynnie roaming about keeping an eye on him. She claims she hates dogs, but seems entirely too curious about the lycan.

He scribbles down idea after idea in a black notepad, and I offer no arguments when he shows them to me, nor do I commit to any.

I'm finally able to shoo him off during our first break in the morning rush. He has a pet funeral to conduct, and Marlena seems relieved when he leaves. She's consolidating trays and refilling napkin holders. "Are you sure he doesn't have a crush on you?"

I get to work on making tree lollypops, one of the treats we'll be giving out tonight. "Don't be ridiculous. He's like an older brother."

As the green candy begins to harden, I insert the white sticks. My godmother carries a stack of napkins past me on her way to the stockroom. "What's he wound so tight about? Did he feel the upheaval in magic like I did?"

I haven't explained everything to her, and I want to discuss my mother's missive, but I start with the earlier issue. "He's upset about Torren's visit last night."

She makes a face. Wynnie meows as if seconding her distaste. "What did the bloodsucker want? You never did tell me. Did he pay for the new stove?"

"New stove?"

She points.

I hadn't even noticed, but there it is, all shiny and modern. Good gumdrops, my mind has certainly been elsewhere. "I can't accept this," I say, even as I caress the knobs.

"The fridge is still a pile of junk," she says.

At least he didn't go overboard.

She points up at our second-floor apartment. "More to the point, do I get to bring Gunther out? He's itching to spill blood."

"No drawing blood. I'll have a talk with Torren. Maybe I can figure out a payment plan." It really is a lovely stove.

Malena grumbles. "So why is Cyn upset about Torren's visit?"

I use a spatula to scrape the last of the green goo from the bowl. My plan—unlike any of Cyn's—is simple and straight-forward. Call Torren, put him on the spot about Nightbane, and confirm Cambria has taken out a contract on the ancient one. Then, depending on the target and why my mother is possibly in cahoots with the Undead Nation, either stop said assassin or assist him.

Win-win.

Except I can't in good conscience assist Nightbane or Cambria.

Lose-lose.

"Cyn thinks Torren is manipulating me to be his queen in time for The Guild meeting."

She starts for the stairs. "I'm getting Gunther and taking off his head."

I fly around the table and grab her arm. "You will not. I've got it all under control."

"The Guild is probably responsible for the weird ripple I felt last night."

Or Nightbane is. "You, of all people, know I'm not going to be manipulated into doing anything I don't want. But since there's something going on, I plan to use Torren to figure it out."

As expected, she's disappointed about keeping her sword tucked away. "I never get to have any fun."

"If I need someone beheaded, you and Gunther will be the first to know."

She snags a lollipop, now set, peeling it from the silicon mold and eyeballing the tree. I've flavored them with peppermint, and the scent pervades the space. "I need some action, and while I like the idea of you using the bloodsucker to see what's afoot, I don't like you being close to him. I certainly don't condone you inserting yourself into The Guild. You'll be surrounded by bloodsuckers. All manner of things could go wrong!"

Her appearance in the apron hides the warrior inside. More at home in fighting leathers than ballgowns, she never fit in in Ever After. The reason for getting the boot long before I did is unclear, and she refuses to discuss it, but there were rumors that it involved Lord Spencer, a handsome royal from the Crystal Court in the Shimmering Isles. A place of beauty, the isles are also deadly, and a magical barrier was erected a millennium ago to keep the beasts that roam there from invading the rest of the realm.

Since no one would ever speak of it, and the King and Queen exiled her when I was only ten, I can only guess at what happened. The only scenario that makes sense to me is that Marlena defied my parents to see Lord Spencer, crossing the barrier and unleashing one of the monsters. When I was young, I imagined her fighting the beast and slaying it, but because of her defiance and the jeopardy it caused, my parents sent her here.

Unfortunately, she doesn't seem to fit in well in this realm, either.

At least her curls have relaxed with all the talk about beheading.

I tap my pendant. "I can call Onyx to stir something up for you," I tease, trying to take her mind off The Guild. The gargoyle warms in recognition.

Marlena chokes. "You will not! That beast will fry us all."

Onyx sometimes struggles with his fire control. "He did fine at Halloween when he helped take the kobolds back to Ever After," I remind her.

She waves me off with a towel, her gaze now avoiding mine. "So what is this plan of yours?"

I relate what Torren asked of me, but go light on the potential peril, leaving off the prophecy and Nightbane altogether. "He needs me to investigate Cambria. See if I can uncover what she's up to and put a stop to any interference she's planning with The Guild meeting."

"Sounds like you might need me and my baby."

I don't, but she's like Cyn—they both want to keep me safe. I might be able to distract him, but she's a whole other candy apple. "You just want to whip out that sword."

Her grin is bright enough to light the shop. "Jo likes it when I show him my moves. Did you see him this morning?"

"I did. He said to tell you hi."

"Will he be upset if you help Torren with this? We agreed to stay neutral with supernatural affairs and keep our noses out of their business. Plus, for us to continue assisting Outcasts, we have to stay out of the spotlight."

I can handle the mayor. "He'll be on my side if he finds out what's going on."

"There's more to this than you're telling me, isn't there?"

I stammer, caught in the omission. "Isn't there always when it comes to the Undead?"

She seems to brace herself. "Seraphina. What *is* going on?"

Moving the lollipops aside, I begin gathering ingredients for our popular chocolate raspberry cupcakes that are on our list for today. "Since we have a new oven, we might as well use it." I set the temp and press the button, enjoying the cheerful beep it makes. "Bake while we talk."

We fall into a comfortable rhythm of mixing batter and filling tins, while I provide details on everything that has transpired since Torren's midnight visit, including my mother forcing me into a bargain.

I have to hand it to Marlena—she withholds comment until the end, although her opinions show openly on her face. When the last tin is filled and the oven has signaled the temperature is right, she slides the pans inside and wipes off her fingers. "Cambria is an evil witch who believes Nightbane is real. She's hired an assassin—whose name and details we don't know—to kill him, but Torren wants to protect Nightbane and has asked you to help him. In the middle of it all, your mother has commanded you to work with him. Did I miss anything?"

"That pretty much sums it up."

"No wonder Cyn is troubled. This is like playing with dynamite. I don't see how helping the Undead helps the rest of us, but not stopping Cambria could also end in disaster. What is your mother up to?" The question is asked with such intense seriousness, it confirms my own trepidation about the Queen's involvement. "Do you believe she knows about Nightbane?"

"Let's assume she does, but why would she intercede? She cares nothing for the magical beings of this world."

"Not to speak ill of her, but...perhaps she intends to expand her territory. She *does* love power, much like the blood-suckers. Is it possible there's more to this Nightbane than you've uncovered? Does he possess the kind of power she seeks, or does she see him as an adversary in her way to gaining it?"

I set the timer. "That's what I need to find out. If this prophecy is nothing but a myth, she wouldn't care about the strife between the witches and vampyres."

"She either wishes to use Nightbane, partner with him, or destroy him, for her own purposes," Marlena begins washing bowls. "What is he exactly? Part Undead and what else, do you think?"

"Not sure."

"Demon? Angel?"

She's left out the one possibility that frightens me more than either of those. "What if he's one of us?"

Her curls tighten. She hadn't considered that. "The ripple." Her hands scour the stainless steel with fury. "I'm telling you, you better talk to Jo."

"I need more information about Nightbane first, and details about the assassin hired to slay him. Whoever that is must be powerful in his or her own right if they can do such a thing. Keeping the mayor out of it for now gives him deniability with the town council. He may be an angel, but he's still our leader and his neutrality is crucial to Enchanted Haven."

And if Nightbane is what I think he is, even a fallen angel won't be able to stop him.

But will I?

Chapter Seven

A line of apples rests on wax paper in front of me. Five have been dipped in caramel and decorated with green sour candies. Five are 'poison' apples that sport tiny skulls.

Yes, it's Christmas, but I'm in a peevish mood.

The last five, I'm dipping in white chocolate and they will be covered in hot cinnamon pieces as part of my fire-breathing dragon line.

Onyx is a gargoyle, but he approves.

I sense Torren's arrival, and my mood lifts when he attempts to break a fresh ward I've placed on the building and fails. Marlena closed the shop at seven and did the cleanup. Her warning to be careful of my mother's assignment and its pitfalls echoes in my ears long after she heads for the town square for the tree lighting. She doesn't care about the ceremony, but she's meeting the Outcasts there before she transports them out of town.

The new ward zaps the vampyre, and through the bay window, I see it set him back on his heels. Golden stars from my magic shimmer around him. They're pretty and remind me of home.

This is my home now, I tell myself.

We sold out of all the lollipops and most of our other holiday-themed treats. I'm happy over the fact we delighted kids and adults alike, and I might have enough to cover the bills this month.

But I'm sold out for tomorrow, so I missed the lighting in order to work on inventory. I'm disappointed and conflicted—creating sweets is necessary for business, and yet, I was looking forward to the experience. A part of me feels like I let Betty down.

Creating an opening in the ward, I call through the doorway, "You can come in now."

When he enters, he appears properly chastised. As always, his magic is deliciously tantalizing, and he is as handsome as ever in a black suit that matches his obsidian eyes. It's a challenge for me not to lick my lips.

"In all my years," he says, stopping a few feet away, "I've ever encountered a witch such as you."

Probably a good thing, considering the only ones like me are in Ever After. "How many years is that, exactly?"

He studies me with bemused eyes. "You wouldn't believe me if I told you. I'm ancient."

Like Nightbane? "The master vampyre status denotes that. Humor me, oh ancient one. How old are you?"

"I was created before the time of the man called Christ."

I pause in dipping another apple. "Holy popcorn balls." Even my kind doesn't last that long, although time moves differently in my world than here. "What is an elder like you doing in this small town? Don't you have some ostentatious castle in the 'old country' to hang out in?"

He points at the new stove. "I assume this commercial version better meets your needs?"

I bite my cheek at his redirecting the topic. "Yes, it's fine, but please don't buy me things in the future. We're going to work out a repayment plan, too. Starting the first of January."

"You needed a new one, and I had the means to provide it. I know your funds are tight and that your magic must be used sparingly. I'm also aware of what happened when Marlena attempted to repair the previous one last week. The two of you do a great service to this town, and I'd rather you didn't go up in flames."

I swallow the image that creates, remembering Izzy and that nightmare. Marlena and I did attempt to fix the previous oven with only a sprinkle of magic, and it resulted in a fireball the size of a troll. "Thank you." I can't be ungrateful. "But the repayment plan starts January first, understand?"

"You are a fiery one," he says and smolders.

Fudgsicles, I hate—*love*—when he does that.

I clear my throat and force my attention back to the dragon apple. "Tell me about the being Cambria wants to assassinate."

"You don't need the details." When I glance up, his eyes have lost their smolder and he's a statue. "Suffice it to say Cambria's target is valuable to the Undead."

"If you expect my help, you can't keep me in the dark. If you fear me finding out about Nightbane, why ask me to take care of the problem?"

His preternatural stillness ratchets up a notch, and the hair on my arm snaps to attention. "You know about Nightbane?"

I decide to act as though I know it all. "Why is he such a secret?"

He relaxes slightly. "He? Ah, I see." He paces, and his cognac and caramel scent becomes overpowering. "Believe me, if I thought someone else could handle this, I would not put you in danger. It is your particular magic that I suspect will be needed to protect Nighbane. Something as ancient as mine but more unique."

That didn't answer my question, but I must be patient. "I'm certainly older than people think, but not that old!" I huff and roll the candy-coated apple in cinnamons. The contrast between the red and white is pretty. "Power aside, you came to me because I have no affiliation with any local coven. Cambria doesn't even know my name, much less consider me a threat."

A twitch of his lips confirms it. "That does work in my favor." He glances toward the exit. "Your watchdog is sleeping on the job, I see."

I warned Cyn to stay away if Torren showed up. "I don't need protection." The clock shows nearly nine, and I need to make good on my promise to stop by the open house. "Either tell me about Nightbane or leave."

"I'm bloodbound to secrecy, I'm afraid, but I can share the reason the witch is after *him*."

There's a message between those words. If I can pin down Cambria or the assassin and make them talk... "Spill the candy, but make it quick. I have an appointment to get to."

"I shall accompany you. We'll discuss it on the way."

"No." I remove my apron and hang it near the door to the office. "Tell me now."

Irritation flares in his aura, but he suppresses it. "While the Undead seek to expand our territory and rights, Cambria seeks to weaken us and reduce our status in the supernatural community to slaves."

"What does expanding your territory and rights entail?"

A predatory grin is his response. "If you would like to be

brought into the inner circle, I can arrange it. It would be my pleasure to make you my Queen."

Back to that. "I'm not the type." I grab my jacket and leave the apples to finish setting. "Here's the thing—I can pretty much stop anyone or anything, but I have some non-negotiable rules."

He steps toward me, eager. "Name them."

The smoldering eyes are back, as is his flirtatious smile. It's all I can do not to move away, and equally hard not to throw myself at him. "Do you know who the assassin is?"

"I do not."

Truth. "Tell me who the assassin is after and why."

His face goes stoic once more. "You must bond with me or become part of the inner circle to be privileged to that information."

You have to give him credit for sticking to the party line. The clock says three minutes to nine. The open house will be over even if I start for City Hall now. I'd hoped to work the truth out of him, but that will have to wait.

Good thing I grew up in a royal court and know a thing or two about getting my way. "I know about the prophecy."

That's all I say, just dropping the bomb and watching his reaction. Absolutely nothing changes in his demeanor.

Gotcha. His non-reaction tells me I'm onto something.

Still, I need to play it cool. "I'd say it was fun talking to you, but it wasn't." I motion for the door. "Goodnight, and good luck with your assassin dilemma."

He doesn't move. "What are your other demands?"

Hand on the doorknob, I have to think fast, as I didn't actually have any. "I work alone—no interference from you or The Guild."

"Not possible. I'm in charge of keeping Nightbane safe. I'm duty-bound to work with you on this mission. What else?"

Curses form on my tongue. "You suck—and I mean that literally and figuratively—at the art of negotiation."

He grins, showing his fangs to punctuate my joke. As he walks to the door, the fangs disappear, and he's inches from me. I have to look up to meet his eyes. "What else? What do you require to accept my offer?"

His very male predatory presence is doing strange things to me. Onyx warms my skin. My mother has duty-bound me, too, but I must use what leverage I have to get him to talk. "Doesn't matter." My voice comes out huskier than I'd like. I clear my throat. "You won't meet my first two."

His eyes do that thing that makes all my lady parts sit up and cheer. I feel him trying to get past my personal protective magic.

I kick him in the shin, fling open the door, and shove him out. "Stop it! You can't mesmerize me, or use your magic to put me under thrall. I'm not that kind of supernatural, and you know it."

He brushes at his pant leg as if dirty from my shoe, then adjusts his jacket, chuckling. "Yes, but what exactly are you?"

I close the door behind me and lock it. We all have our secrets. "Just a candy store witch," I assure him. "One who can't help you."

Chapter Eight

I hustle for City Hall, checking my watch. The night's nocturnal animals serenade me as I pass the Whispering Pages Library with its dark windows. The sky overhead is awash with stars and a nearly full moon.

What am I going to do about my mother's order? I consider and discard multiple options as I continue past the quaint shops, the Victorian street lamps illuminating chilly fog rising from the brick walkway.

"Seraphina Fairchild, is that you?" I glance across the street to see Maude sweeping her stoop of new fallen snow. The Trumble Dentistry sign in the shape of a molar glows white behind her. "Hi, Maude."

She stops, annoyed that I don't address her as 'Doctor,' like the rest of the town. She's generally irritated with me, since she attributes my sweet shop to the downfall of humanity. Without human cavities, I ask you, where would she be? "Feeling better?"

"A-okay."

"Where are you off to?"

"I promised Betty I'd stop by the open house. Did you attend?"

She smiles in response, but I'm not sure if it that's a yes or no. "You're running a touch late, aren't you?"

"I'll help her clean up. I'm sure she could use an extra pair of hands. Want to join us?"

That shuts her up. She takes her broom inside, throwing a weak, "Have a good night" over her shoulder.

She handed out toothbrushes on Halloween and warned kids to stay away from my shop. If she were Santa, she'd stick toothbrushes in stockings as presents.

Torren appears out of the shadows. "I do not care for that one."

"Geez!" I jump, hand flying to my chest. "Are you following me?"

"You left our conversation unfinished."

I start walking again, glancing back to see Maude watching us through the window. She quickly steps away, but the glowing tooth spotlighted her clearly.

He also checks the dentistry's window. "She doesn't care much for you."

"She doesn't care much for you, either, and our conversation *is* over."

Still, I have to admit, I'm secretly pleased— if he's continuing his attempt to recruit me, he's ready to bargain.

"I spoke with Kaile. We are amenable to giving you more details."

"Kaile? Is he a vegetable?" I tease.

I know who he is—sort of. After a greedy vampyre tried to usurp Torren's reign at Halloween, Kaile sent me a formal thank you note with a bouquet of two dozen blood-red roses.

He's the North American King of the Undead attending The Guild meeting.

Torren falls into a graceful step with me, giving me a chastising glance. It makes me once more feel a bit like prey. "There must be a formal contract in place in order to do so since you are not my queen yet. I am to escort you to the Omni Hotel for the signing."

Yet. He's as determined to make me his partner as I am to never wear a crown.

We near the municipal parking lot next to City Hall, my shoes catching on the ice-covered blacktop gravel and making a scratching noise. A few residents linger at the Witchy Wishing Well to drop in a coin or two before heading home to tuck in for the night. A lone car sits under an old oak in the corner of the lot, a sprinkling of the day's snow on the roof and hood. Betty's still here. Good. "Tell me I don't have to sign it in blood."

The vampyre chuckles, the low sound making the tiny neck hairs stand up. "Would that be so bad?"

"No blood contracts," I say, stepping onto the sidewalk. Betty will chew me out, but I have an excuse—I'll blame my delay on Maude. "And while the hotel is considered neutral ground, walking into an unknown meeting with a vampyre king, isn't my sweet tooth. I'll pick the time and place."

He opens the door for me. "You have nothing to fear. I'll be with you."

I frown, not because I'm skeptical, but because the sign has been flipped to the closed side. "Did you just unlock that?"

"It was already so."

I step through. "Betty?" I call.

The interior is shadowed with only a dim illumination

filtering out from the back. Torren sniffs the air and stops me in mid-stride. "Something is amiss."

It sure is. Onyx flares to life, but I'm unsure if it's because of Torren's touch or something more sinister. As I follow him to the source of the light, we pass Mayor Jo's office, locked up and dark, and stop outside Betty's. Her door is cracked a few inches, and the tension in Torren's body puts me on edge. I attempt to slide the door farther open, only to have him block me.

"What is it?" I ask, resisting his attempt to shield me.

"Betty?" he calls. "Are you here?"

There is no response, and he takes his sweet time opening the door wider. A wash of magic rolls out over us, and instantly, my own bursts out in a sparkling bubble.

Well, that's new. I touch the reflective colors of it, a since of awe and wonder momentarily distracting me from the threat that prompted it.

The vampyre lifts a brow in question. "As I have mentioned, your magic is—"

"Unusual, I know. Sometimes it even surprises me."

Under her open window, Betty is slumped in her chair, arms thrown wide. Her face is frozen in a startled expression, her eyes unseeing. Stuffed in her mouth are several of my strawberry Santas.

"Your scent is all over her," Torren states.

All I smell is the faint odor of pine and snow drifting in through the open window. "*Mine?*"

He checks for a pulse in her neck. "You were here earlier?"

"This morning. I brought..." I point to the protruding fruit. "Those."

A trail of juice trickles down Betty's chin.

"She is alive," he says, "but barely."

I have, unfortunately, seen other dead bodies. I'm relieved Betty doesn't fall into that category.

"Her pulse is languid and flat. Her blood flows, but slowly." His dark eyes are concerned. "It seems as if she's in a type of stupor. A trance?"

Her skin is cool under my fingers. "Like the Undead kind? Has she been put in thrall?"

A shake of his head. "Not like that. This is...unusual."

His choice of that word puts me on edge again. "You think *I* did this?"

"Of course not. But you have to admit, it's alarming that your scent is all over her, your strawberry Santas are stuffed in her mouth, and her condition suggests an odd supernatural-induced stasis."

A fissure of fear snakes through me. I've been behind jail bars before, and I have no intention of going there again. I check for bite marks, and seeing none, I pull out my phone. "I'll call an ambulance."

Even as I dial, my gut tells me he's right—this has faerytale traces all over it. After I complete the call, I remove the fruit from her mouth, hoping that might act as a catalyst to free her.

"Should you disturb the scene?" Torren asks. "You mustn't assume she reacted to your strawberries."

My nose scrunches as a wave of dark magic leaves her open mouth. "The Santas had nothing to do with this. It's not an allergic reaction." Her elf hat is on the floor behind the chair. I pick it up, dust it off, placing it on the desk. "Kiss her."

Torren blinks and stares at me as if I have lost my marbles. "I'm sorry, it sounded as though you told me to kiss Betty."

"I did." I point to her berry-stained lips. "I'm working a theory."

"What exactly would that be?"

His reticence to do my bidding annoys me. "You're right—she's in a magical coma. It's been noted that a kiss can undo that sort of thing. Since you're the only available male in close proximity..." I point at her lips. "Don't skimp. Make it a good one."

His disbelieving scrutiny continues. "Faerytales again. You realize they are fiction. Imaginary."

"Of course." If only. "Humor me."

In the distance, the wail of sirens cuts through the night. "I'm no Prince Charming."

You got that right. "You're the only substitute I have at the moment, and as humans say, beggars can't be choosers. We need to know who did this to her and why. That means we need to wake her up. A kiss might do it."

His face does interesting calisthenics as he considers the proposition. "Giving out nonconsensual kisses is not my standard MO."

"Glad to hear it. Think of this as...first aid. If she were bleeding and you had a bandage, you'd apply it, right?"

"Perhaps blood is not the best analogy."

"Right." I snap my fingers. "What if she were choking? She wouldn't be able to ask for help, but you'd certainly know she needed it."

He schools his features, gives me a reluctant sigh, and leans forward to place his lips on hers.

He starts to pull back, and I press his head down, making sure the contact lasts longer. When he finally rises, batting my hand away, we stare at her, holding our collective breaths.

"Betty?" I snap my fingers in front of her face. "It's Seraphina. Can you hear me?"

Nothing. She's totally catatonic.

The vampyre seems both pleased that he was right and

disappointed that his kiss didn't create a miracle. "Her pulse increased briefly," he informs me. "Perhaps she can sense we are here, and a master vampyre of my lineage kissed her."

I pinch my lips together and try not to roll my eyes. The magic that hit my nose smelled strongly of oranges. That's the stuff of Black Heart Court magic, but how can that be? Elves, in particular, who pride themselves on doing the dark queen's bidding. I've seen a few of Ever After's kind here, but not elves.

"Can you drop one of your enchanted candies in her mouth?" he asks. Or cast a wake-up spell?"

"To make such a candy would take time and a spell might make things worse." I chew my bottom lip.

"Think of it as first aid."

"Don't be cheeky." I toy with the hat, wondering if her choice of costume has some underlying connection to this. "Fine, I'll try." I shut my eyes and piece a few lines together. *"Awaken now from your sleep, as I cast this spell, may your slumber retreat. As I speak these words, let them ring true, awaken, dear one, I summon you."*

We wait, anxious. She doesn't even blink.

Torren guides her head forward, examining the back of her neck. His eyes lift to mine with a disquiet that makes my stomach knot. "We have our answer."

The siren draws closer, their sharp blare screaming in the open window.

Leaning closer, I examine her neck, where he has moved her hair out of the way. Now I'm confused. Two deep puncture wounds ooze the color of the berries. "But you said—"

The ambulance brakes at the curb, red and blue lights slipping into the room.

"No vampyre did this." Torren uses his phone to snap a picture.

A man hollers from the front. "First responders! We're coming in."

"Back here," I call. I lower my voice to him. "What did, then?"

He returns Betty's head to its original position, and we both step aside as the EMTs rush in. "Shifter," he mutters under his breath in my ear. Goosebumps travel down my spine. "A wolf, to be exact."

Chapter Nine

Time was creeping toward midnight when the police, including Buck Barnhill, our new chief, was satisfied that neither Torren nor I had any hand in Betty's condition.

Buck is one hundred percent human but married to a witch. He understands a few things about magic and the world at large, never takes anything at face value, and reminds me of *vrumines* in Ever After—big, slow, and clever under his flat stare and saggy jowls. Similar to Minotaurs in human legends, *vrumines* also love labyrinths and solving puzzles.

"I don't need to remind either of you that this district has been deemed *neutrum*." He glances around to confirm no mundanes are in hearing range. "If I find out she was attacked by a supernatural, I will personally show him"—his gaze pins Torren before switching to me—"or her the inside of a jail cell. Do I make myself clear?"

Torren meets the accusation with an air of ease. "Neither of us would violate the treaty."

Buck is overly suspicious of me because of the Santas, and

Torren by association. "He's right—we had nothing to do with this, nor do we know who did."

The chief glares at us in a final warning. "You two take care, and Miss Seraphina?" His old-fashioned manners are common in this part of the country. "I expect you to be more judicious about the company you keep." Another glance at Torren.

I bristle at his parental tone, but it's mostly due to the fact I'm upset. Getting on the wrong side of the chief is a recipe for harassment, so I paste on a smile. "Don't you forget to pick up some chocolate truffles for Carmen, you hear? I made fresh tonight."

His wife is a die-hard chocoholic. She claims my candy enhances her spells.

He tells me he'll be by first thing, and I vamoose, not caring if Torren follows.

He does, of course. "Add Barnhill to the list of folks who don't care for you," I say.

"He doesn't even know me, but vampyres and witches don't get along, so naturally, he sides with Carmen."

Mayor Jo rests against his car across the street, arms crossed. He straightens as we near. "You want to tell me what's going on?"

He's come from the hospital. I can smell the scent of disinfectant and pharmaceuticals on him. "How's Betty?" I ask.

"No improvement." His focus lands on Torren and narrows. "What are you doing here?"

"I was with her when she discovered the body. I'm lending emotional support."

"Can either of you explain why my office manager is in a coma?"

"I'm sure the chief will figure it out," I assure him.

"Where's Malena?" he asks. "She left right after the lighting. I was going to buy her a hot cocoa."

"Oh, she was planning to go to bed early. We've been swamped, you know."

He studies me, as if suspicious of my indirect lie.

Torren holds out his phone with the photo of Betty's neck. "The markings suggest a wolf did it."

Jo eyeballs the picture. "A bite?" His icy blue eyes lock on Torren's.

The accusation in them doesn't unnerve him one bit. "The indentations are canine." He uses his fingers to enlarge the shot. "Anyone familiar with magical creatures can see that."

The dig makes the mayor's forehead crease. "I suppose the next thing you're going to tell me is that Cyn is involved."

"It appears to be lycan," I say, "but Cyn is innocent."

I feel the tickle of his angelic magic brush against me. Yep, he knows I'm keeping things from him. "How do you know?"

A theory is taking shape in my head, but it's much too soon to share. I couldn't, even if I wanted to. I hurry to find a logical reason to defend the shifter. "Cyn would never repudiate his standing in the community and risk being banned by violating the treaty."

Jo thinks this over. "Why would a wolf target Betty? Why would anyone, for that matter?"

That's what we have to find out, but we can't meddle in Barnhill's investigation. "I don't know, but she's lucky we arrived when we did. Bite marks aside, the coma might have turned deadly if we hadn't pulled those fruits from her mouth."

Both males fix their attention on me with expressions that suggest I've said too much.

"Is that so?" Jo asks.

Oops. "I smelled oranges when I removed the fruit from her lips. The magic our culprit used was poisonous, and the fruits kept it from escaping. I'm assuming it may have been fatal if we hadn't found her."

Jo makes a 'huh' sound. "A wolf who used poison to incapacitate her and then bit her?" We both nod. "You think you scared him off before or after he got what he wanted?"

"The window was open," Torren tells him, warming to the idea. "He may have gone out that way when he heard us arrive."

I nod in agreement. "There's no way to know what he was after, but I doubt it was solely Betty's...demise." I shove the phone back at Torren. "I don't know why Betty was the target, but whoever did this may come after you, too. The attack may be tangled up with the politics of our town or the treaty."

"Or The Guild?" he adds in a suggestive voice.

Torren is still unrattled. "Seraphina is right. You should be on alert and take precautions for your safety."

There is a long pause as the wheels in Jo's mind spin. "Could someone be after my job?"

"With no angel to enforce the treaty," Torren says, "the town could fall into maleficent hands."

"True." I pat Jo's shoulder. "We don't want that to happen."

He narrows his keen eyes at me. "What aren't you telling me, Seraphina?"

I like Jo. I don't want to be on his bad side any more than Barnhill's. Plus, Marlena will be upset if I do anything to perturb him. "I don't have concrete proof, but I have a theory. Let me look into it and get back to you. I promise, if I find out anything, you'll be the first to know."

His feathery magic tickles me again. The majority of

magical creatures can't sense it, but I'm most. I hold still, pretending I don't notice, even when Onyx gets twitchy.

After a few heartbeats, he relents. His distress over Betty shows in the set of his jaw. "You have my permission to use whatever means necessary to figure it out." He pauses to let that sink in. At Halloween, he tasked me with an investigation into a murder suspect, and I used magically-infused candies to do it. I nod at the inference. "But I expect regular reports."

"Of course." I offer a reassuring smile. "I'll do my best not to interfere with Chief Barnhill's investigation but get you the answers you need."

"As will I," Torren adds.

I turn on him. "You will not."

His eyes glint with roguishness.

The mayor opens his car door to climb inside. "Good luck losing your sidekick, Seraphina."

Torren turns haughty. "I am no lowly sidekick."

I snort. "He's *not* my sidekick."

As Jo gives us a half-hearted wave and leaves, I grab Torren by his cashmere coat and haul him a few feet away. The chief and his officers are also leaving, bright yellow crime scene tape securing the area.

I want to ditch the vampyre, but he might have the information I need. He's more familiar with this realm than I am, and there's the bloody bargain with my mother. Assessing the sleeping neighborhood, I assure myself we're alone. "I know why the attacker bit her there. He tapped into her spinal fluid."

Torren removes my hand and brushes at his sleeve as if I have wooly aphids. "My assessment as well."

I start toward the shop. "Why would he do that?"

A night owl calls to us as we pass under a giant oak near the town park. Torren's shoulder brushes mine as we walk side by side. "To access information." When I shoot him a look, he adds, "Spinal fluid carries memories. Some vampyres will do the same when they need knowledge."

The breeze chills my neck, and I flip up my collar. "What would Betty know that this creature wanted?"

"I don't believe it was a werewolf. While it's unlikely Cyn is involved, a shifter is the culprit."

"I don't think it's a shifter, per se."

"Then what?"

I could be wrong. I hope I am. "I think it's a witch who purposefully uses magic to turn him- or herself into an animal."

"Metamorphosis?"

I nod, my insides as chilled as my skin. If this is who I think it is, thanks to the orange scent, she's not any ordinary witch. She's from the Black Heart Court. "Cambria's hired an assassin that's the best around."

"I had assumed so. The wolf and the assassin are the same?"

I rub my arms, trying to warm myself through the material. "I once knew a family of evil magic workers with the ability to transform into such creatures. They used the same method to retrieve information that aided them in thwarting their enemies."

He looks slightly relieved. "Then you must know how to stop this one."

The owl hoots again, and the haunting sound crawls down my spine like a furry spider. "I do," I tell him. "Unfortunately, stopping her isn't that simple."

"Her?" His happiness returns as he regards me with an air of confidence. "Together, we can handle anything."

If only that were true. My mother's orders make sense now. "Time for you to bow out." I stop on the corner of Cyn's church. "Not only because it might violate the covenant for you to actively work on this, or because your sidekick status is in question." I wink, but my attempt at levity doesn't amuse him. "Seriously, this job is all mine."

Not even the streetlamp is able to lighten the dark depths in his eyes. "Whatever you are hiding from the others, you need not do so from me. I have not survived for over two thousand years without having seen and heard it all."

A part of me longs to tell him—tell *anyone*—just to get it off my chest. Exile is no joke, and I miss my family—yes, even my mother—and my original home. This place has welcomed me, and I'm determined to make the best of it, but I only have Marlena to talk to about our kingdom. What's it like to be *Outcast.* Weak moments sneak up on me.

Plus, there's the prophecy that could help me clear my name, and I'm still convinced that the only way I can do so would be to return to Ever After. Which is out of the question unless I clear my name first. It's a spiraling maze that I can find no way out of.

Weakness means vulnerability, and far worse if I violate the terms of my exile. "I appreciate your offer, but there's nothing to tell." *Nothing I can tell, anyway.*

He surprises me by not arguing. "How long do you need to refresh yourself?"

"What?"

He checks his watch. "Kaile awaits us at the hotel."

"I told you, I know who the assassin is. I don't need to be brought into your vampyre circle. I'll take care of the problem, no payment necessary."

He stares at me, expressionless. "There's bad blood between you and this assassin, isn't there?"

That's putting it mildly. "There's nothing for you to worry about. I've got it all—"

My words are cut short when the scent of oranges hits me, followed by the owl. Shrieking with menace, it dives for my face.

Talons swipe at my cheeks, feathers whack my hair. Onyx flares to life, and another of those shimmering bubbles engulfs us.

The owl hits the shield and goes tumbling head over tail-feathers. It screeches again as it flaps away into the night, leaving behind a single feather that floats to the ground at my feet.

Torren grabs me. "Are you all right?"

Stroking the red-hot gargoyle at my throat, I speak soothing words. "All is well, my friend." The bubble fizzles and slowly dissipates. "Fine," I tell him. "That was no ordinary owl."

I'd give chase, except it has disappeared, and while I have some pretty cool powers, flying isn't one of them.

Torren retrieves the feather. "Why did it attack?"

I take it from him, eyeing the pattern. I have another theory. "I'll find out. Goodnight."

He keeps pace with me as I head to the back door of my building. "You're not giving me the brushoff."

I stop, sighing. "I told you to let it be. I can handle it, and I don't need your help."

"Clearly, you can protect yourself. However, this situation involves someone dear to me, and I will not be shoved aside. We can stand here and argue, or we can work together and solve this mystery."

Is he talking about Nightbane? Why would that creature be dear to him?

Cyn bolts from the church wearing tartan pajama bottoms and matching. short-sleeved shirt. "I heard shouting and screeching. What happened?"

Torren waves him off. "Nothing that Seraphina and I can't handle. Go back to your den."

"Not on your Undead life." He races across his lawn and over to the door. "Tell me what's going on."

Great, now both of them are crowding me.

Keeping my irritation at bay is pointless; it's like arguing with a *vrumine*. A softer approach might work. "I appreciate the two of you looking out for me since I arrived here. You've become good friends. Tonight, however, I need peace and quiet to think." I give them a tired smile. "There is indeed a lot going on with Christmas, The Guild, and what happened tonight with Betty, but—"

"What happened with Betty?" Cyn interrupts.

"She's in a magically induced coma, and Torren can bring you up to speed. Right now, I need to work on something, so please excuse me."

Before I can shut them out, they each shove a foot across the threshold. "We're not leaving," Torren says.

"One way or the other," Cyn adds, "we're coming in."

If I don't mainline sugar in the next thirty seconds, I'm going to kill them both.

"Tell Cyn about Betty," I order Torren as I snap on the lights and snatch a caramel apple from the front case. Torren gives a huff but does as requested, answering Cyn's questions as I consume the fruit in several large bites.

"You've got..." Torren gestures at the corner of my mouth.

I lick caramel from the crease and then wipe my lips. Scooping up a handful of candy toadstools from a glass jar, I down those next. The sugar hits my bloodstream a heartbeat later, and I sigh with relief.

A modicum of patience returns, and I grab my black cauldron from its hiding spot. Marlena is still gone, and maybe that's for the best. Otherwise, I would have three hovering helpers. Placing ingredients into the black iron bowl, I heat it on the stove. When the liquid boils and steam rises pink and yellow from its surface, I drop in the feather.

The vapor goes grey, and a ghostly form materializes. Her face is hard, angry, and powerful.

"Oh, snickerdoodles," I murmur.

The two males step forward, one on each side of me, to get a better look.

"Who is that?" Cyn asks.

"Is that the witch?" Torren adds. "She's the owl, too?"

I wave a hand through the face, dispersing it with a shot of sparkling energy. "The owl is her psychopomp."

Cyn pivots, a frown on his face. "Psychopomp? Like, they take souls to the afterlife?"

Torren frowns. "But you would have to be dead for the owl to do so."

"Exactly." I back away from the cauldron and snatch up a handful of decorated marshmallows from another jar. Cute snowman faces smile at me before I eat them. "She's powerful, deadly, and...," *bent on revenge.* I swallow the words. "I'm doomed."

Chapter Ten

The next morning, Marlena and I begin work at five. She has that look in her eyes that I know well. "I can't believe what happened to Betty. It has to be tied to this situation with the assassin. You need to step carefully, and I'm bringing out Gunther, whether you like it or not."

"That's a good idea."

She stops in her work of sprinkling powdered sugar on fresh pastries. "You're agreeing with me? Are you running a fever?"

I make a face. "I need to tell you what Torren and I discovered." I fill her in on Betty's bite marks, our theory, and the owl attack.

When I tell her who I saw in the steam, she gapes. "That's not possible."

"That's who I saw. My reveal spell never lies."

Working helps her think. It does me, too. Together, we stew over this disconcerting news as we mix and bake and frost. She calls Jo, and he updates her on Betty—there's been no change.

It hadn't been easy getting Torren and Cyn to leave the previous night, but when I threatened bodily harm, they relented. Cyn offered to stand guard, and although I assured him my wards were impenetrable, the light in the church alcove stayed on all night. He was watching the building, ready to pounce should we need him.

Torren lurked in the shadows until dawn. While invisible to the eye, I sensed him checking my magical barriers for weak spots that could be breached.

He didn't find any, but every time he poked at the ward, it sent an alarming zap straight to my chest, waking me from my already troubled sleep. I considered marching out there to threaten his Undead life, but in some weird way, it made me feel safer having him there. Cyn too.

Dangerous territory. Outside of Marlena, I can't let anyone get close, or allow myself to depend on them. Even her crush on the mayor could be a problem.

As is our custom, the two of us sit for a cup of refreshment before opening the shop. Marlena pours peppermint cocoa for us, then snags a spice bar for her breakfast. I nibble on a sugar cookie decorated like a reindeer.

"It can't be her," I say, breaking the silence. "I must have mistaken her features for her mother's."

Marlena eases back in the white chair, a match for the small café table. She's as dumbfounded as I am. "Someone could have brought Izzy back to life."

"In this world? No one has that kind of power, not even Cambria, and how could she know about Izzy in the first place? Even in Ever After, a dark witch would need Izzy's DNA to work such magic. It has to be Veramis."

Veramis Ravenswood, queen of the Black Heart Court, is Izzy's mother. The last time I saw her, she made it clear she wanted revenge on me. Bringing my friend back to haunt me— a challenging feat for anyone, even her—might be the most clever vengeance I've witnessed in all of my years.

Marlena picks at her bar, taking a sip of the cocoa after each bite. She claims it's the perfect combination of bliss. "Who knows what Cambria can do? Maybe she's learned of Outcasts and is working with one to increase her powers and dabble in necromancy. Or she crossed into Ever After, retrieved one of Izzy's bones, and..." She shakes her head. "I don't know."

The cookie no longer appeals. I put down the uneaten face. "No one but a royal can raise the dead, and only the Black Heart Court manipulates the laws of life and death."

Our eyes lock over our treats. "Your mother would never work shadow magic."

"Veramis would. I smelled oranges on Betty's breath."

Marlena sets her cup down hard enough to spill her drink. "She can't leave the realm without your parents' permission, and they would never give it to her."

"Monsters have slipped through to this world before. It has to be Veramis." I'm uncertain if I'm trying to convince myself or Marlena. "My mother discovered her plans to send Izzy after Nightbane, and that's why she's ordered me to work with the Undead to stop her."

"Or..." She hesitates a moment too long.

"Or what?"

"There's no easier way to take over a territory than to turn enemies against each other. While the vampyres and witches are busy fighting, the Queen could swoop in to crush them all." Marlena spins the cup in its saucer with her invisible magic. "But logically, it seems more likely Veramis. I don't believe she's used necromancy, though. It would alert your mother and put her court at great risk. Much easier to create an imposter to haunt you."

Marlena doesn't realize I see spirits. Could it be possible that Izzy's *ghost* has followed me to this realm? The idea is both terrifying and compelling. Perhaps I don't need to return to Ever After to unravel the mystery behind her death!

My godmother frowns. "Are you all right?"

"The ripple you felt the other night...could it be from Veramis creating this imposter?"

She tilts her head. "It was dark magic, that's for sure."

"Could have been necromantic in nature?"

"Yes, but like I said, that would unbalance this world and Ever After. Your mother would know if Veramis tried it, and she would send her soldiers after her. Veramis would never risk that."

"But if Veramis works with Cambria, she never has to leave Ever After to do it."

Her eyes spark with understanding. "Cambria could be her vessel." She shakes her head. "This is bad. Really bad."

Another thought that's been digging into my brain demands I give it credence. "Maybe Izzy never died."

Marlena blinks. "But your memory..."

"Has been tampered with. I'm sure of it."

"How?"

"I don't know, but it's possible someone only wanted the kingdom to think I killed her." The clock on the wall in the shape of a candy house dings the hour. It's time to open. I stand and push in my chair. The partially eaten reindeer smiles at me. "Either way, I must prepare for any and all possibilities."

"*We* must prepare." Marlena rises as well, gathering the cups and plates. "What's our first step?"

Through the front windows, I see a line has already

formed, customers anxious for their pastries. The shop smells of freshly baked goods, and I inhale, appreciating all that we've accomplished in such a short time. "What we always do—sweeten the pot."

Marlena grins as she dons an apron. "Oh, goodie. I'll get Gunther sharpened."

Cyn is first in line, waving at me from the other side of the door. *Bad shifter.* What am I going to do with him?

"Ready?" I ask Marlena. When she nods from her station behind the display case, I flip the lock, and our day begins.

As the morning rolls into the afternoon, my thoughts become more focused, thanks in part to my candy toadstools, which I keep a steady stream of in my system.

During a pause in customers that afternoon, I stroll into the backyard. The garden we've outlined for a spring planting is not much bigger than a certain pumpkin carriage of faerytale fame. The oak and apple trees have lost most of their leaves and have been trimmed with holiday lights, thanks to the goblin children whose parents are Outcasts like us.

The Outcast community often pays homage to me. Shy and reticent, the children leave baskets of fruits, vegetables, and tiny replicas of people and animals made from twigs, spider webs, and acorns in the yard. They can be seen peeking out from behind bushes and tree trunks but disappear as soon as I wave at them through the window or walk out to say hi.

A single red apple dangles from a low-hanging branch. I pick it, and say to the tufted titmouse on the fence. "I request the service of the goblin, Trinken."

The bird is barely bigger than the apple, but she has magic in her and scoops it from my palm. Her wings beat the air, and she and the red splash of fruit disappear into the gray afternoon.

Requesting a powerful goblin's assistance is risky, as he will exact a high price, but he has a legendary sweet tooth and can be paid off with the right candies.

I'm not one to sit back and wait for my enemy to make the first move, but walking into Cambria's territory unprepared is ill-advised. While she isn't more powerful than I am, she is smart, and I must abide by the *neutrum* or risk eviction from Enchanted Haven. If Veramis is using her as her vessel, she may be equal to me in magical ability. She's more familiar with the environment, people, and places here, and to eliminate her, and the threat she and Veramis bring, requires stealth and cunning.

Whether one of them has raised Izzy from the Otherworld or created a likeness of her to sabotage me, I need my wits. On a scale of one to ten for evil, the Black Heart Queen ranks one hundred. Partnering with Cambria is a strategic move—one that could be deadly for all of us.

A brief late afternoon rush forces thoughts about Izzy, Veramis, Betty, and the others to the back of my mind. Shortly before closing, a woman enters, and Marlena calls me to the front.

Marlow Livingston looks like she is straight out of a faery-tale in the starring role of the evil stepmother. Her dark hair is swept straight up, and her full lips are glossed to blood-red perfection. Her wool suit is designer, and so are her three-inch heels and giant tote. Veramis Ravenswood would either peg her as a friend or a fierce competitor. "Seraphina," Marlow purrs with her refined drawl, "I heard about poor Betty."

Marlena busies herself refilling a giant glass jar with gumballs, but I know she's listening to every word. She's as suspicious as I am about this visit. "Did you need candy for stuffing stockings?" I ask.

Her smile becomes sardonic. "Oh, heavens no. The

Livingstons don't do stockings. We go skiing in Aspen for the holidays."

Heaven forbid, I suggest something so mundane. "Then what can I help you with?"

"With Betty in the hospital, the Chamber needs someone to handle the details of Santa Fest and the Reindeer Scavenger Hunt."

Her goal for this visit becomes clear. "And you're the next in charge, right?"

Her tote, the size of a beehive, swings from her arm as she steps closer. "Well, I can't be expected to handle it. We leave first thing tomorrow for our trip."

"If you're suggesting I do it, I'm sorry, but no. We"—I point to myself and Marlena—"are part of the scavenger hunt."

Her long nails click on the countertop. "Surely Marlena can handle this place on her own."

My godmother steps to my side. "We're expecting several hundred kids through here that night."

Plus, we may be hunting a couple of no-good witches and an assassin. "I'm sorry," I state firmly. "It's out of the question."

She winks at me as if I'm playing hard to get. "The Chamber would be extremely grateful, Seraphina, as in, we'd owe you for your service."

Lady Wynnie meows from the kitchen; a clear warning not to give in. *I know*, I tell her. Then to Marlow, "Why don't you ask Cyn to do it?"

Her smile falters. "The preacher?"

The bell over the door jingles and Mayor Jo walks in. "Afternoon, ladies."

I hope he's bringing news about Betty, but he points to the

lone red and white ribbon candy in the case. "Can I get that to go?"

Marlena slides out the tray and puts the peppermint in a bag. Her smile makes her look twenty years younger. "Would you like anything else? We have a few turnovers left."

Marlow interrupts. "Mayor, I was just recruiting Seraphina to supervise Santa Fest and the Reindeer Scavenger Hunt."

"I can't," I insist.

"No worries," he says. "I've already spoken to Maude about it."

"Maude?" Marlow and I ask in unison.

He nods. "She's got a way with kids. She jumped at the chance."

"*I* have a way with kids," I say. I don't want the job, but Maude? Really?

For some reason, Marlow seems equally distraught about the dentist, but before she can argue, a well-dressed man holding a red apple strolls past the window. His head turns, and his gaze locks on mine through the pane.

"Who is that?" Marlow asks.

The dark hair, simmering eyes, and tall physique don't fool me, but she is instantly enthralled.

Trinken continues on and disappears around the corner. Jo is instantly on alert and ready to follow. "I've never seen him before."

"He's a gardener," I say, motioning for the mayor to stand down. I give him a subtle wink, hoping he catches on that this is part of my covert investigation. "I called him to have a look at my rose bushes. They have a fungus."

"In December?" Marlow asks.

"Gee, look at the time." Marlena comes to the rescue. She flies around the case and hustles all of them to the exit.

"Seraphina and I have a ton of orders to fill tonight, and it's already after closing."

"But I haven't paid," Jo argues.

"On the house." The bell goes off as she shoves them out.

Once the door is locked and the sign is flipped, she whirls on me. "Do I want to know why there's a goblin posing as a GQ model in our backyard?"

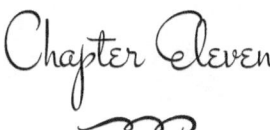

Chapter Eleven

"Your Royal Highness." Trinken gives a half bow, the apple in hand. "How may I be of service?"

Due to the fact I'm *Outcast*, he doesn't have to pay me respect, but since he's been on the receiving end of my mother's ire and sentenced to the same fate as me, he must feel a certain camaraderie.

That, or he's being ironic and poking fun at my very non-majestic existence. Hard to tell with goblins.

"Sir." I dip my chin, showing him equal respect. "Thank you for meeting with me. I know you didn't have to come."

His eyes take on a silvery cast. "One day, when we both return to the realm, I hope you'll remember my loyalty."

He wishes to go back. I can't blame him. If his hope is that I'll be his ticket to return and that endears him to my cause, I'll play along, "You and your family will be favored among all goblins."

His magical façade flickers, showing his true form: large nose, pointed ears, and equally pointed teeth. "I will require a more substantial gift for any favor I perform."

"Of course." I expected as much. I don't have room to negotiate, but seeing as my intentions don't ever see me sitting on the palatial throne, I can promise a whole bunch of treasure on the condition it comes from the royal coffers. Plus, I'm counting on my enchanted candies sealing the deal. "I need you to set up a meeting with a witch in this world named Cambria. Are you familiar with her?"

He looks down his nose. "I know all the magical creatures of this world. She holds great ambition."

She's not the only one from that silvery gleam in his eye. "The meeting must take place in the fringe territory." It's a border between this world and Ever After; a hazard zone where Outcasts often attempt to breach the wards of the kingdom to sneak in. "I'm requesting your permission to do so, as well as asking for your help in coercing her to speak to me."

His clever eyes narrow. "Forgive my inquiry, but why?"

Veramis seeking revenge on me, or raising Izzy for the same purpose is one thing. It could be more. The Shadow Queen can't leave Ever After, but what if she's offered Cambria a chance at crossing the border into it? My mind whirls in directions I'd rather it didn't, thinking of what might become of my people. Like we don't have enough wicked witches running around, causing havoc. If Cambria entered Ever After to join forces with Veramis, my mother and father would never stand a chance.

Sneaking a toadstool, I give myself a jolt of sugar, and then offer him one. He's going to need it.

He accepts the treat and listens as I outline my theory. I finish with my request. "I want to negotiate a bargain with Cambria."

Out of everything I've said, one significant fact has caught his attention. This shocker is enough to make him lose control of his glamour. The homely goblin face peeks through once more. "The Princess Isabella lives?"

"I don't have proof, but certain facts point to it. It may only be her ghost, but we must be prepared for any possibility."

His focus drops to the apple. "Who could restore her to life?"

"The one person in the Black Heart Court who wants retribution for her death."

His face turns ashen. "You do not mean....?"

"Yep." I need to get him a cookie or something more substantial than the toadstool before he passes out. He suffered greatly at the hands of the Shadow Queen. "I suspect the person who raised her is none other than her mother."

When my negotiations with the goblin are completed, I return inside. I have promised him a lot for his cooperation, but if he meets his end of the bargain, he gets a hefty payout of gold if I'm ever welcomed back to the faerytale land of our birth, and while we're stuck here, a lifetime supply of my sour punch gummy bears.

I got off easy.

Marlena fixes dinner, and we eat while discussing my plan. In order for Veramis, Cambria, or Izzy to dole out malevolence, they'll kidnap me, or attack those closest to me in order to terrorize me.

Marlena will make sure they don't.

Veramis is as clever as the goblin, but so am I. To get what she wants, I'm betting Veramis created a bargain with Cambria to destroy Nightbane. A bargain that is full of deceit and deception. If I can convince Cambria the bargain will only succeed at getting her killed, not Nightbane, perhaps I can sabotage Veramis.

As my godmother and I discuss the possible scenarios,

Onyx trembles with excitement. I see it in my godmother's eyes, too—action and anticipation ripple in the air, as heady to them as sugar is to me.

"If we use magic in the fringe, the sentence is death," Marlena reminds me.

"Which is why we must capture Cambria going in or coming out. I don't like making her my prisoner, but it's the only viable option to get her to listen and ruin Veramis' plans."

"Take the pawn off the board. Be sure you have plenty of candy bespelled with lock and key magic."

A summons arrives, my bird messenger pecking at the back door. On the stoop, I find the apple, one bite missing—the goblin's signature on our bargain. The titmouse lands on my outstretched hand, a slip of paper in her beak. I read the details: Quadrant six. One turn of the clock hands.

Pocketing the paper, I take a bite from the apple, feeling the bargain spark to life. Swallowing, I return the half-eaten fruit to the bird. Her tiny claws grasp the stem, and she flies away to return it to Trinken, the pact between us sealed.

"We're on," I call over my shoulder to Marlena.

"For what?" Torren appears in front of me.

Cupcakes and frosting, what is he doing here? "Nothing, go away."

"You're planning to stop the assassin?"

"Yes," I admit. "By stopping Cambria. Your problems will be solved."

"I will accompany you."

"No opening for a sidekick on this mission."

His face remains unemotional, but I see a tick near his left eye. "You should not handle this alone."

"She's not." Marlena emerges in her leathers, tucking her

sword into its sheath on her hip. "I'm her sidekick. Get lost, bloodsucker."

This provokes a reaction. "You are in sore need of an upgrade," he says to me.

Gunther flashes, nearly beheading him, but the vamp has lightning-quick reflexes. The blade zips through empty air. "Not bad," he says to her, straightening his tie.

"Back at you." She leans toward him as if sharing a secret. "Just so we understand each other—if I'd wanted your head, it would be rolling around like a bowling ball right now."

"Your prowess with the sword is exceptional."

I feel a 'but' coming and step between them to diffuse the tension. "You're both amazing and skilled." The apple piece in my stomach contracts sharply and then begins to pulse. Time to get a move on. "When I've defeated Cambria, you're welcome to resume your competition. At the moment, I must go, and Marlena is my partner for this."

Torren falls into step as I walk. "One sentinel to guard your back is inadequate."

Marlena snorts her annoyance.

My apprehension grows rather than lessens at his insistence. "Torren, I know you mean well, but you are *not* equipped to handle what I'm about to face."

"Cambria cannot overpower me."

"She's not working alone, and her conspirator can."

He gives a nod, not because he believes it. No, this is more of a pat on the back, like a master to an apprentice. "It is good you expect the worst and have planned for it."

A cloud floats across the moon. I scan the sky and trees for any sign of the owl—or a ghost. All is quiet. The apple tracker in my belly is not. It grows more intense. The fruit that

Trinken possesses works like a homing beacon, pulling my feet forward. "I'm a strategic thinker."

"I find that alluring."

A laugh bursts from me, from nerves as much as from his statement. We cut through the graveyard behind the church, the portal to the fringe growing closer with each step.

To my dismay, the screech of a screen door opening and its solid whack, as it slams, echoes across the quiet landscape. "Where are you going?" Cyn calls. In a heartbeat, he's on my other side.

"By all that's magical," Marlena mumbles. She is behind us, making sure no one sneaks up on me. "Why won't you two leave us be?"

"We're just out for a walk," I tell Cyn.

He glances over his shoulder at my godmother. "Brought your sword for a stroll?"

A husky voice whispers through the dark. "*I'm no ordinary sword, Barren.*"

The shifter stops and pivots to face Marlena. He points at Gunther. "I swear that thing said something."

I grit my teeth and glare at Marlena. "Really? Now? Great timing."

The blade rarely speaks, preferring to ignore the world. "*I'm not a thing, you canine moron!*"

We all come to a stop, and Marlena grins. "My sword's name is Gunther."

Cyn's gaze flicks my way, and I shrug. He scratches the back of his neck. "Ahh...okay. Nice to meet you, Gunther. I've never met a talking sword before. I'm not a baron, by the way. Just a man of the cloth."

"Not baron," I clarify. "*Barren* is a not-so-nice term used for the people of this realm."

"This *realm*?" Torren echoes.

I'm so frustrated, I've let a key detail slip. "Help," I whisper to my godmother.

"She can't talk about where we're from or our kind of magic, so don't ask, or you'll endanger her life," Marlena states and scoots around the males. "We don't have time for you and your questions anyway. Run home, boys, and let the big girls handle this."

The two of us leave them standing there stunned into silence for the first time since we've met.

Chapter Twelve

"Do you think that worked?" I murmur, kicking away dead ivy from my boot. It covers the ground in patches not covered by snow.

Marlena doesn't get a chance to answer. Cyn and Torren appear in front of us, blocking our way and nearly scaring the frosting right out of me.

"We're accompanying you regardless of our *inferiority*," Torren says. "We are not without skills."

"Dude, I never said I was inferior," Cyn mumbles.

"*Well, you are, dog breath*," Gunther tells him.

Cyn looks unnerved. "Look, ...er, sword... I don't know what your problem is, but—"

The apple piece in my belly burns. "Please! If I tell you a story, will you let us pass?"

Marlena shoots me a quelling glance. "You can't."

"It's just a story," I assure her with a wink. "A faerytale."

Torren moves aside. "I wish to hear it." He motions for me to lead the way.

I keep my feet planted. "No interruptions, no questions."

"Agreed."

Cyn nods.

I motion at Marlena, and we resume walking. "When we get to the portal, the two of you must promise to leave and return to your homes."

Snow crunches underfoot, neither of them agreeing this time.

"Explain the term 'barren,'" Cyn says, his wolfish eyes glinting in a patch of light cutting through the canopy. "Why is our world labeled that way?"

"Because humans are barren of magic." I say. "Yes, you have vampyres, shifters, witches, and other assorted beings, but the magic where we come from is...different."

"You're pushing it," Marlena growls under her breath.

A voice comes out of nowhere. "What you all are doing out here?"

My head snaps up. Mayor Jo sits on a branch high up in an old oak tree. "Mayor?"

He leaps, landing gracefully on his feet and causing a plume of snow to go airborne. "This is a surprise."

Marlena stands straighter. "We were out for a night stroll. What were you doing in that tree?"

"Beautiful night." He takes her hand and bows over it, giving her a subtle kiss. "Isn't it?"

She giggles. Giggles! He didn't even answer her question.

"It's cold, if you ask me," I say.

"What update do you have for me?"

I gulp. "I'm working on it right now."

"Hmm." He regards me and the group. "Chief Barnhill isn't having any luck with his investigation. I was hoping you were."

"I am." Sort of.

Torren sidles up to me. "*We* are. I'm sure after tonight, we'll have key information for you and the chief."

Jo nods and puts an arm around my shoulders, guiding me forward again. "Assorted beings. That's what you said, right? Like me, you mean?"

The chill in my bones dissipates with his touch. "You're also unique, but not like us. Magic in this realm comes from a source outside of each of you. Spells, the elements, that sort of thing. It also requires certain resources to keep you... powered up."

Torren is unhappy about Jo's arm around my shoulder. Quick as lightning, he knocks it away. "Explain."

Jo glares at him. The vampyre ignores it.

Oh, good grief. "You're a vampyre," I say to Torren, "created by another vampyre. That creation occurred because of an exchange of blood. Blood continues to sustain you and give you powers."

"And me?" Cyn asks.

"Your essence is blended with animals, giving you their abilities. You also have certain dietary needs, as well as the need to shift regularly."

"Angels are from God," Jo says, a touch of superiority in his voice.

"All religions have beings they call divine. Your existence relies on human belief."

"Seraphina." Marlena's tone holds a warning.

Torren glances at her and then back at me. "Agree to her terms," he tells Jo, "so she will tell us the story."

I raise a questioning brow to him, and he nods.

"Okay," I say. "Once upon a time...."

"In a galaxy far, far, far, away," Cyn interjects, chuckling.

Everyone groans.

"Sorry," he says. "Wrong storyline."

"Similar. Not a galaxy, but a different dimension," I state.

This pleases him, and he smiles, his white teeth shining in contrast to the shadows on his face.

"Please refrain from interrupting again," Torren snaps.

I take a deep breath and launch in. "There was a golden kingdom ruled by the gracious King..."—I must create fake names for my characters, as well as the courts—"Oswald and his enchanting Queen Jessamine. There was bounty and good fortune for all, even in the Night Court."

Cyn starts to say something, but a look from Torren silences him.

I go on. "The Black Heart Court, full of all sorts of shadow beings and led by Isorena, signed a peace treaty with the Golden Kingdom, profiting handsomely from it. All lived in harmony."

A rabbit appears on the path, a beady eye zeroing in on me. I feel no ill intent but wonder if it's one of my mother's spies. I must be careful.

As we enter a clearing, I turn left, following the tug in my belly. The rabbit bounds into the woods. "The king and queen had a daughter, a princess, who was one day destined to take the throne. Because of the treaty, she was allowed to roam the kingdom freely, never fearing any harm.

"She was known for her notorious sweet tooth,"—Torren cuts his eyes to me—"and as a young girl, she often snuck into the enchanted forest to eat delicacies she'd stolen from the castle's kitchen, where the most talented of bakers worked."

While I keep my voice steady and level, my nerves are jangling the closer we get to the portal. I need to hurry this story along. "In the forest, she met another princess, one destined to a similar fate. One princess of light and one of shadow. The two girls found they had much in common—including their love of candy. Together, they used magic to create a cozy cottage entirely from their favorite treats."

My audience seems enraptured. I notice Jo has fallen back to walk next to Marlena. Her face is screwed up as if she's sucking on a lemon drop and her eyes are hard and disapproving about my trick.

Some stories can't be rushed, and I slow my steps, the gravity of tonight settling deep in my stomach next to the apple. "The girls became the best of friends, meeting at the cottage whenever they could escape their parents. One day, the shadow princess was upset, her training now moving to the dark arts that her mother, Isorena, insisted she learn. One of the princess's tutors let it slip that the princess had a pre-ordained fate— to someday crush the royal family and rule over the Golden Realm."

A piece of dead ivy snatches at my ankle, causing me to stumble. Torren catches me. Even the plants are my mother's agents.

Nerves tingle up and down my limbs, painful as pin pricks. I now have three entities to keep safe, and I'm about to meet up with the most powerful witch in this realm, in league with Veramis. "The golden princess didn't believe in pre-ordained fate, convincing her friend that she could create her own destiny, choose her own path."

An owl hoots above us, the zing of Marlena's sword rings in the frigid air. But the owl simply lifts off, vanishing into the sky.

"I take it the golden princess had to eat those words?" Jo asks.

A sharp pang of grief zaps my chest, and my breath falters. I swallow the lump in my throat and begin walking again. "She did indeed. Two of her other friends, a brother and sister, were at the cottage one day. The golden princess had built a great fire in her fireplace and then gone out to find more wood for her stove. The Black Heart princess showed up, upset about something of great importance to her. A fight broke out, and she used dark magic. She tried to kill the brother and sister. Things got out of control."

Cyn's face lights up. "Wait, I've heard a similar faerytale. The brother and sister wouldn't happen to be—"

"Shh." This time, it's Marlena who shuts him down. "We're out of time. The Black Heart princess died. It was a tragedy. Our true nature cannot be overcome, nor can our fate be avoided. The end."

"What happened to the golden princess?" Torren asks. I can hear it in his voice— he has put pieces of my faerytale together with their real-life components.

A woman comes crashing out from a copse of trees, out of breath, with leaves in her hair, her jacket askew. "I want to know, too! What happened to the golden princess and her friends? What about the king and queen? Where's the happy ending?"

I squint. "Maude? Have you been following us?"

Jo crosses his arms. Cyn shakes his head in disgust. Torren schools his face into a blank.

The dentist straightens her coat, looking cornered. "I… uhh…my cat got out. I was chasing her and saw you walking through the graveyard."

"I didn't know you had a cat," I say.

She focuses on Marlena. "That's quite an outfit." She points at the sword raised in the air from my godmother's surprise, moonlight causing the blade to glow. "Are you going to a costume party? Or are you into that cosplay stuff? My niece goes to the fair every summer. She likes to dress up like a peasant woman."

"You're lucky I didn't cut off your head," Marlena grouses.

Maude laughs, uncomfortable. "You really get into character, don't you?"

The apple twinges. I'm not sure what to do about yet another uninvited guest, and time is forcing me forward. "How did you not sense her?" I grumble to my godmother.

"I was scanning for *magical* entities," she fires back. "Not mundanes."

I scan Maude myself. "No magic."

"Not a drop."

At least she's not a spy scouting for Cambria or my mother.

"Want me to kill her anyway?" Marlena offers.

All three males look shocked. Their gazes land on me.

I chuckle nervously. "Don't be silly. Torren, would you escort Maude back to town and wipe her memory?"

"I am not leaving you," he counters.

At the same time, Maude draws herself up to her full height, which is still several inches shorter than the rest of us. "*Wipe my memory*? Is this more cosplay?"

"You can do that, right?" I ask the vampyre.

A tilt of his head. "It's a skill I possess."

"Then do it. My safety could depend on it."

"Why?" Cyn asks.

"No one is doing anything to me!" Maude adjusts her coat again, bravado in the lift of her chin. "You guys are nuts! I know my niece can really get into character, but come on." She eyes Torren. "Why aren't any of you in costume like Marlena?" As if it dawns on her that all is not well and that

86

there is not a mock play, she steps back. "What's really going on?"

"I'm not leaving you," Torren states again. "Maude won't speak of this to anyone, will you?"

His gaze locks on her, and a sudden burst of magic tugs at the hair on my arms, tingling my skin. Her body relaxes, and she smiles. Her eyes, reflecting Gunter's glow, grow fuzzy. "Whatever you say, Master."

Cyn makes an exasperated noise. Maude sways on her feet but stays rooted to the ground, completely under Torren's mind control.

Marlena lowers Gunther. "Keep her that way until you can wipe her memory," she orders. She points at the path. "Let's go."

We start hiking with Maude now part of our caravan.

"She doesn't have a cat, does she?" Jo asks.

Cyn glances at me. "So what *did* happen to the golden princess?"

Ahead, I see the glow of the realm magic around a giant billboard with 'Welcome to Enchanted Haven!' on it. My stomach contracts. The portal.

There's enough enchantment to steer normal folks away, keeping all but the chosen from entering the fringe. "That, my friend, is a story for another time." I move forward and raise my hand to a pumpkin in the center of the sign, Marlena following. Magic, cold and sharp, bites the skin of my palm. "You must now hold up your end of the bargain and return home."

Torren starts to argue; Cyn shakes his head, and then both Jo and Marlena snap to attention, their gazes locking on the trees behind us.

Marlena raises her sword. "Too late."

Following their line of sight, my royal blood ignites and Onyx sears my skin. Dozens of elves emerge from the woods—they've been waiting for us.

I expect Cambria, or perhaps the Queen of the Black Heart Court herself, to appear. Shifting like liquid shadows, the being who emerges from behind an ancient rowan tree is neither. "Hello, Princess," Izzy says. "Miss me?"

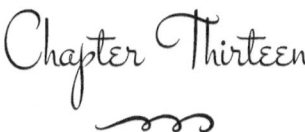

Chapter Thirteen

"Izzy," I choke. "You're alive."

"She was cloaked," Marlena says, "along with her minions. I couldn't sense her."

I swallow the lump in my throat. If this is an illusion by Veramis, I'm a sucker. I want to throw my arms around my friend. Beg her forgiveness.

"Surprise!" Her eyes are not filled with mercy but with loathing. Dark magic pours off her.

Steadying myself, I search for the best way to handle this. If only I had a candy for securing forgiveness. "I'm sorry. I never meant to hurt you."

"Right. That's why you killed me."

My friends take a collective gasp. "It was not intentional, no matter what your mother or anyone else believes. You're the closest thing I've ever had to a sister. I love you."

Her laughter is menacing. "We both know that's not true. We were born to be enemies."

"How is it possible that you're here?"

She whirls, her skirt flaring around her ankles. "Black magic feels good. You should try it."

So Veramis *has* raised her. "Necromancy is against our laws. Your mother shouldn't trifle with such things." And my mother should know she has.

"I thought you'd be happy to see me." Her voice is rich with irony. "The Crown Princess cast out of Ever After and living among humans." She *tsks.*

My secret is out now. I avoid the others' stares. "I miss home, but I like it here. I have more freedom than I ever did in our realm."

"All those years trying to convince me to turn my back on my natural, inborn gifts." She slinks toward me, and everyone stiffens. I hold up a hand to keep them from doing anything rash. One of her long nails traces its way down my cheek, and I notice a blue sigil on the back of her hand. "How did being the good girl work out for you, *sis?*"

She hisses the word, and my heart clenches. We were as close as sisters. Of all that's missing in my world, perhaps that's what I miss the most. "We should talk."

Her laugh is devoid of humor. "I didn't come here to talk."

What she did come for is evident. My magic rises, Onyx itching for the command to descend on my old friend and burn her to a crisp.

Been there, done that. Accidentally, but still.

I can handle her, I assure my guardian, *and Marlena can fight the elves.*

I think.

If it were the two of us against them, I'd feel more confident, but now I have four others to worry about. While each of them, with the exception of Maude, has magic, it's not enough to protect them from the evil princess and her army.

"Did you leave Cambria at home?" I ask, searching for a diversion.

Izzy licks her lips, "The witch was tasty. Her power delicious."

I didn't expect this, and a different kind of understanding dawns on me. "This was never about the vampyres and their prophecy, was it?"

Maude steps out from behind Marlena. "Are you going to the costume party, too?"

Izzy does indeed look dressed for the part. She flicks her eyes to the dentist and back across the angel, vampyre, and lycan. "You've certainly lowered your standards since your banishment."

So she knows about that.

"Hey, there." Jo moves forward, casual as a fox, holding out a hand. "I'm Joseph, mayor of Enchanted Haven. I'm sure we can work this out. Just tell me what it is you're after."

A grim smile parts her lips, her gaze landing on my face again. "You didn't tell them?"

The only way to save my companions is to get them into the fringe. Unfortunately, it's forbidden to non-magical people.

I have no choice. I place a hand on the billboard's center. "I was getting around to it."

Torren is beside me in a blink, facing Izzy. "If you have eliminated Cambria, we have no quarrel with you. If there is something you wish to negotiate, that can be arranged."

I appreciate his attempt at an intervention. Her smile becomes amused. "Negotiate? That's cute."

The malevolence rolling off her, regardless of the smile, makes my teeth tingle. "Your quarrel is with me. They have no involvement in any of this."

She prowls toward Cyn and traces a ringed finger down his arm. "They'll all be mine soon enough."

He gives her a lazy smile as though he welcomes her touch. Then, quick as lightning, he snags her wrist and jerks her to him. His smile turns feral. "Be careful what you wish for, witch."

At the action, the elves step forward in unison. Marlena flashes her sword in a warning.

Izzy snaps her fingers with her free hand, halting the elves. She leans her face closer to Cyn's. "I like lycans. All that animalistic nature ready to come out."

Maude slides behind Marlena once more, peeking over her shoulder. "Excuse me, but I'm not with them. Heck, I don't even like Seraphina— or whoever she is." Slowly, one step at a time, she walks backward, putting distance between herself and the rest of us. "She rots kids' teeth with all that candy she sells. It's terrible." *Step...step.* "I'll just be going. My cat is waiting for me. I've got to get home and feed her. You know how demanding felines are." She picks up her pace, starting to jog as she waves over her shoulder.

I reach deep into a pocket, keeping my other hand on the portal.

"Stop," Izzy orders, jerking out of Cyn's grip. I'm not sure if she's talking to me or Maude. "You're not going anywhere."

Maude freezes, and with another snap of Izzy's fingers, she's transported back to us. She screeches and flails into Jo. With attention on them, I withdraw a handful of faery dust and bring it to my lips. "Don't be so sure of that," I say, and then I blow.

The sparkling particles land in her eyes. The dust covers her and the elves. While they swipe at it, I lasso my friends with a thread of magic, yanking all of us into the fringe.

"They can't be in here!" Marlena yells, her sword still raised as we land in the soft, cotton candy band surrounding the fringe.

The pastel border reminds me of Saturn's rings. It filters out the unwanted and protects the enchanted. It also harbors creatures who have fallen from the queen's favor but have not been exiled. Acting as a sort of jail for them, they live in the hope she may find favor with them again, and their sentence be reduced or eliminated.

Barren cannot cross into it...unless someone with my abilities and bloodline transports them here. "It'll be okay," I assure her.

It's so *not* okay.

Trinken is here, expecting me and Cambria, not the host I've brought. "I'm afraid I disagree." He wears his human form, but the female goblin next to him—his wife Hookba—is all ears, nose, and stubby appendages. Her skin is a dust grey, wrinkled like an elephant.

"Your Highness." She curtsies low, her bird-like nose nearly touching the ground.

"How lovely to see you again," I say. It's been a long time since she was sent here after Trinken was exiled. I don't even remember for what either of them did.

As is the custom in the kingdom, when she raises her gaze, her eyes don't quite meet mine. I see joy in them that I remember her. "We are honored to assist you on this mission."

Trinken points a very straight human finger at the swirling vortex of the portal. "This meeting is only for you and Cambria. Your deception is a breach of our bargain. Return the *Barren* to their rightful home."

Maude swipes a hand across the energy of the fringe, glittering dust coating her fingers. "This is some hangout." The dust releases a warm vanilla scent into the air as she sniffs the pink coating. "Is this cotton candy?"

Before I can stop her, she licks her fingers.

"Stupid *Barren*." Marlena mumbles.

Maude's eyes roll up in her head, and she faints. Jo rushes to her side. "What just happened?"

Cyn and Torren, with their stronger survival instincts, take a step away from the walls and the now-sleeping woman.

"She'll be alright in a few minutes," I assure the angel. I turn to Trinken. "I seek sanctuary for my friends."

Marlena and Hookba both suck in a breath. This is no small request.

He glares at me. "I cannot grant any such thing. You know the laws."

"I do, but Princess Isadora Ravenswood brought an army of elves." I raise my hand, closing the portal even though it is the goblin's duty.

He blinks. "She's dead."

"Not anymore, and she claims to have eaten Cambria! If you don't grant sanctuary, she'll eliminate innocents and strike me down."

This changes everything, and he knows it. Our bargain is null and void. "I assure you, Your Highness, this will not be tolerated."

"My friends are in mortal danger. If you kick them out, their blood will be on your hands."

Hookba wrings a strip of cloth covering her hips. "But, we have no power here. We cannot be held responsible—"

I feel the bubble before it materializes; no pixie dust to warn me this time. The Royal Crest explodes in front of my face, and fairies dance about my head, touching my hair, clothes, and hands.

The Queen's face appears. "Ambrosia? What are you doing here? You are forbidden from entering Ever After."

She felt my presence the moment I crossed into the fringe but didn't realize who was with me. The connection only shows her me and she doesn't see them.

Time to stand my ground. "I'm carrying out the bargain with the vampyres that you ordered me to. The assassin after Nightbane is here and has brought an army of shadow elves."

Her face contorts. "I know the assassin is there. That's why I need you to handle it."

"Here, as in, right outside the fringe. She seeks to harm me and my friends. I can handle her, but they require protection."

"Friends?" Another contortion. She seems surprised I have any.

"Yes, the vampyre you instructed me to work with is one of them."

She schools her features into her normal stoic face, realizing how much she has given away—the very information she forbade me to share with anyone. I suspect I'll still be blamed. "Why must you always break the rules?"

Some rules need to be broken. "Did you know Izzy is alive?"

While her face doesn't change, I see her chest move with a sharp inhale. "That's not possible."

"It's true," Marlena says, sidling up next to me.

"She's the assassin," I tell her. "Veramis used necromancy, then sent Izzy to humandom to work with Cambria. That witch is now dead at Izzy's hands." My stomach roils at the thought that my friend actually ate the witch. The princess I knew would never do such a thing, but she's no longer that girl. "It seems Veramis' plans reach far beyond eliminating Nightbane."

Splotches appear on the Queen's perfect skin. "Raising the dead is...Veramis would never... I will bring the kingdom down on her head!"

"How will you do that when she's no longer residing in your realm?"

Her eyes snap, fire and ice at the same time. "Do not speak to me with that tone."

Or what? She'll exile me? "We have to work together, Mother." I'm not sure what to do about Izzy and Veramis. What I *am* sure of is that Veramis' interests go beyond vengeance. "We have to stop them. If they amass more power, they could take over this world and yours."

Mother's lips compress into a fierce line. "I will not stand for this."

"Allow my friends to stay here while I speak to Izzy. Maybe I can make her see reason or discover what her mother is up to."

The queen is silent for so long that I wonder if our connection has frozen. I'm about to ask Trinken if there's a glitch when she finally speaks. "If the Queen of the Black Heart Court has raised her daughter from the dead and sent her to that realm, you are indeed in dire straits. She will use you to conquer it."

My friends exchange nervous glances. "Conquer how?" Cyn asks. "Like wipe us out or...?"

"Make us her slaves," Torren supplies. "That's what conquerors do."

Mother doesn't even glance in their direction. "They can't take Ever After. Veramis and Izzy are after a far easier target, Ambrosia, and they need you and your royal blood to help them gain it."

I was afraid of that.

"Come home," she says. "I'll lift your sentence."

I've dreamed of hearing those exact words. The longing I've felt to return has been a constant, dull ache in my chest. Yet, I feel torn in half at the idea. Leave Enchanted Haven? Leave Torren?

Her invitation holds no sweetness now. I won't leave my new friends to Veramis and Izzy's evil plans. "I can't. I'm sorry." I place my hand over the portal, opening it. The swirl of magic sucks at my skin. "Take care of my friends, Mother."

I step through, knowing what I have to do.

Chapter Fourteen

A chorus of *no*s follows me through. Marlena and Torren lunge for me. Onyx trembles as I wave my hand over the portal, sealing them in.

Then I face Izzy.

An empty clearing greets me. No array of warrior elves. No vengeful nemesis. The nocturnal creatures in the woods are silent.

Angry clouds blot out the moon and stars. The wind picks up, and snow falls in earnest. I scan the area for magical enemies, but Onyx turns cool against my skin—there's none to be found.

Where did she go? Did she believe her cause was lost after I entered the fringe?

As the icy wind pricks my cheeks, I send out more feelers. The only thing they touch is nature. The trees, bushes, and soil assure me it is only them under the clouds of the approaching storm.

Placing my hand once more on the billboard pumpkin, I open the portal and wave the others out. "She's gone. It's safe."

Marlena descends on me. "What in all the realms did you think you were doing?"

Saving you. "I had a plan."

She gives me the stink eye. "You ever do something like that again, and I'll..." She huffs, unable to finish her threat. I'm her goddaughter, and in our world, that bond lasts for eternity and prevents her from ever harming me. "Just don't, okay?"

The lycan sniffs the air while the vampyre scrutinizes the space with his night vision. Jo simply pats my shoulder. "Didn't realize you had a death wish, Seraphina. Or should we call you Ambrosia?"

"I prefer Seraphina."

Returning to town, questions, theories, and barely disguised accusations fill my ears as we fight the onslaught of a blizzard. Out of all of them, Maude is the only one who says nothing. She is quiet and pensive.

Jo escorts her to her place. Marlena sends Cyn off, assuring him we will be safe. Torren is the last to idle at the back door. "I require a vow that you will not engage the enemy without appropriate backup."

The protection is his steady gaze, combined with his concern, makes my pulse hop. A welcome warmth spreads through my body, replacing the cold that has settled in my bones. "I can take care of myself."

"I have no doubt you are stronger and more clever than any of us." A gold ring appears around each of his irises, and his cognac and caramel scent envelopes me. "A beautiful name, Ambrosia."

A magnetic tug hits my chest. I swallow hard, trying to break my gaze from his seductive one. Those gold-ringed irises hold mine as though there is an unbreakable bond between us. If only he weren't a vampyre...

"Names hold great power." I can't be held accountable for him and the others knowing mine now, but... "Best not to use that one. It can attract danger."

His lips curve as he backs out the exit. "I have never feared danger."

With that, he leaves. Although I've given him no verbal vow, it feels as if he's extracted one anyway.

Overnight, we endure the blizzard, our electricity blinking on and off while drifts form against the building. It is an out-of-the-ordinary event—and one I'm sure is magical. The storm matches Marlena's mood, and the next morning, she grumbles and growls as we bake and fills the display cases for the day's customers.

Once the last of the storm tapers off, a dozen folks brave the cold and snow to pick up our daily special and cup of cocoa. Nothing keeps folks in Enchanted Haven from what they want. Marlena and I don't have time to chit-chat.

On our first break, I call the hospital to check on Betty.

"No change," the nurse informs me. "She just stares into space. Around midnight, we thought she was coming out of it, but she didn't."

Midnight? "What changed about her condition then?"

According to the night shift nurse, she became agitated." I hear her flipping papers. "She even mumbled something."

"What did she say?"

"The note says she said 'switch' or 'witch' and 'am.' That's it."

Switch or witch. Am... Ambrosia? Was Betty tapped into what happened at the portal? "Is her doctor allowing visitors?"

"Fifteen minutes at a crack. Mayor Jo's already been here, and her sister will be here later today."

"Thank you." I disconnect.

"Well? How is she?" Marlena asks.

I fill her in as I wash a tray. "And by the way, I did have a plan last night. I wanted Izzy to kidnap me and take me to her hideout so I could figure out what she, Veramis, and Cambria are up to. It must be nearby."

"You heard what the Queen said. They want you and your power. You would have played right into their evil hands."

A pair of our regulars, Petrina and Karen, interrupt further discussion to pick up orders for the local ladies' auxiliary benefit. A craft show, wine-tasting, and holiday tour of historic houses decorated for Christmas are on the agenda.

Karen helps herself to a sample of my homemade caramel corn. "Booth space sold out in October, but Hannah Martin had to pull out." She points a finger at the front window display. "You should take her place and showcase your gingerbread houses. I bet you'd get orders for a dozen."

Even thinking about creating the many makes my heart clench. Each one echoes the real candy house I built with Izzy when we were still friends—the place I escaped to every day when royal demands at the castle were too much for me.

"There's no time. I'd have to hire extra help," I say, bagging up the Christmas candy they're giving to their members.

"I'll volunteer," Petrina volunteers. "I love making gingerbread houses."

"Good." Marlena whooshes past, shooting me a glaring look. "You're hired, so put us down for that booth."

I give her a surprised look, but she's already headed for the kitchen, her back to me.

"Excellent!" Karen claps her hands. "Yours will be a huge draw. Everyone loves your sweets."

The two exit. I scowl as I tag after Marlena. "Why did you do that? Even with help, we don't have time to add more to our plate. The time to make extra candies alone to do the decorating"—I list the items mentally: *peppermint twists, mocha patties, gumdrops*—"Petrina has no experience with candy-making."

Marlena washes another tray, the spray hitting the metal and showering her in a faint rainbow mist. "Don't forget, raspberry truffles, cherry cordials, Santa suckers..." She continues as though everything is normal, but I'm not listening. *Cherry cordials.*

"You think if I'm too busy with the shop, I won't take on Izzy?" I give a derisive laugh. "Nice try."

She shrugs. "Your call—disappoint your customers or leave Izzy and the others to me."

"Fat chance." One way or another, I'll handle both.

Later, after closing, I grab my cape from the hook at the back door. "I'll be back soon."

"Where do you think you're going?"

"To visit Betty. I won't be gone long." I dump a jar of hot cinnamons in a bag and shove them in my pocket. "I promise to be safe."

The sun is sinking on the horizon as I walk to the clinic, streaks of peach and gold lighting my way. The snow is pretty, but I'm not fooled by its glistening pureness. Like faery dust, it can enchant, and I pray no one will be affected by it. As I walk, I drop a cinnamon every few feet to melt the snow. The children will be disappointed, but at least they won't end up bespelled.

The shimmering dust reminds me of Cyn's jacket. I never did question Torren about his motives.

Motives—the thing that drives all of us.

I'm relieved when no one joins me on the walk. I'm also surprised. Every corner I turn, I anticipate Cyn, Torren, or Jo popping out to catch up with me. Not even Maude makes an appearance.

Inside Betty's room, I touch the flowers folks have sent while I watch a *Get Well Soon* balloon float in the corner. She lays in a partially raised bed, eyes vacant, a monitor beeping softly in rhythm with her heart.

I take one of her cool hands in mine. "Betty, I'm so sorry. I don't know if you can hear me, but I'm going to figure out a way to reverse this, I promise."

There's no response, only the rising and falling of her chest, her features blank.

A slight tickle of magic washes over me. I glance toward the dark corner. As I stare at the empty space, I see the tiniest particles of dust sparkling around a faint outline.

"You can come out of hiding," I say.

An audible sigh fills the room. The ripple expands as Torren takes form. "How is it you can see through my cloaking magic?"

"I don't see through it, per se. Magic creates a residue of sorts. There is no cloak or any form of it that can truly hide from me. If I look for it, I can see it." I return Betty's hand to her side. "You left some on Cyn's jacket the other night, with a dose of catnip dust. Why?"

"I keep an eye on him. He struggles with his sleep, worrying about his parishioners." He straightens his cuffs and flicks his gaze to the bed. "There's been no improvement."

"Did you follow me here, or have you been watching over her?"

"Both. I kept watch after leaving you, but had returned to your shop to check on you a few minutes ago. I arrived shortly after you left, and I followed you at the request of your godmother."

That woman. "Did she give you a choice?"

"If any harm befalls you, she will remove my head—her words—and since she believes at least some of this is the fault of the Undead, I am charged with your health and well-being."

More like she hopes by putting him on this assignment, he'll be the one to end up dead, as in *really* dead. There's no logic to him being able to protect me. She knows that.

I slump into the nearby chair, the worn upholstery stained. The cushion collapses under me. "What can you tell me about death and resurrection?"

His innate stillness kicks in, a subtle frown dancing over his full lips. "What is it you wish to know?"

Behind that frown, I sense confusion and maybe a sliver of hope. I adjust my position, the lopsided cushion resisting the attempt and dumping me off center again. "I don't want to be your queen. I simply want an idea of what Izzy has been through. The mechanics are not the same as becoming a vampyre, yet I imagine some of the sensations, the emotions, and the realization that one has died, only to return, are similar. Does your life truly flash before your eyes as you take your final breath? When you first realized that you were alive once more, what went through your mind? How did your body feel? Did you welcome a second chance?"

Surprised by the flood of questions, he steps closer. "Knowing this will help you how?"

"Maybe it doesn't, but in the realm where I'm from, death is rare. Resurrection is unheard of. I'm curious."

He ventures to the window and stares out. "My brother poisoned me. It was a slow, painful death. Doctors at that time were hacks, but my sister, desperate to save me, went to a more, shall we say, 'unconventional' healer. It was said she studied as a priestess in a long-ago temple. She knew death rights and transformational medicine—a type of alchemy that could remove the poison from my blood and restore my health."

"She was a vampyre."

"No, but to be honest, I cannot say what she was. I've never encountered another like her." He glances over his shoulder at me. "I believe now she may be something like you."

"Believe it or not, I'm not the only one who's been exiled. We're called *Outcasts*."

He gives me a crooked grin, a simple fleeting movement that makes my pulse skip. "She saved me, but word got out. My brother ran away, fearing my wrath. One night, I woke to find a man in my room. I assumed my brother had hired him to finish the job. Instead, I learned the man was a vampyre, building a nation of the Undead. My blood was believed to be charmed, invincible."

"And he wanted it."

A nod. "He became my sire."

"Did you fight him?"

Torren stares outside again. "He threatened my sister. There is nothing I would not do for her, so I gave it freely."

Another question forms on my lips, but the bedsheets rustle. Both of us glance at Betty.

"Her mouth is moving," Torren says.

I launch from the chair, grabbing her hand. "Betty? Can you hear me?"

Her fingers tighten on mine. Her lips tremble.

"It's okay," I tell her. "I'll get the nurse."

I punch the call button, and her grip becomes a clamp. "She's..." It comes out in a whisper. I lean closer.

Torren moves beside me. "You're safe. Do not fear. Help is on the way."

Her head shakes. My fingers are nearly white from her grip. "Here."

"What?" I smooth a strand of hair back from her face.

"She's...here."

The shadow energy hits me just as Betty releases my hand.

"Izzy," I whisper to Torren.

He moves fast as a shadow himself, throwing open the window. In the next instant, he picks me up, rushes to it, and jumps.

Chapter Fifteen

The vampyre jets through the parking lot and into the nearby park, carrying me like a bride.

"Put me down!" I pound a fist on his chest. The muscles there are as hard as steel. "We have to go back and protect Betty!"

"Your safety is my only concern. The evil witch isn't after the human. She's after you." He dodges a swing set, boots crunching in the snow. "If she wanted to kill Betty, she would have done it the other night."

Unless we interrupted her. "Please stop."

He keeps going, the trees a blur. "Not until I'm assured you are—"

I pop a lemon drop into his mouth while it's open.

He nearly chokes. His face screws up. "I...hate... these!"

"Stop running."

He freezes, the boomerang effect nearly ejecting me from his arms. "You are incorrigible."

I stare into his eyes, remembering this—the feel of his arms holding me securely. It would be so easy to fall for him, but I can't, no matter how charming, protective, and interesting he is. "Put me down."

In an instant, I'm free-falling. I land with a grunt on a patch of ice.

He reaches for me, fear on his face. "Your Highness, I didn't mean to do that. Wait...*Your Highness*? Why did I just say that?"

I chuckle, brushing off my pants. "You know my lemon drops force you to obey me. I guess now that you know my bloodline, they also force you to address me properly."

He eyes me with speculation. "I'm unsure whether I find that appealing or annoying."

"Go with annoying." I rub my now aching hip. "The spell needs work on the 'Do exactly as I say part.'"

The candy has not fully dissolved, and he spits out the remainder. "How long does it last?"

I can't hide a grin, liking the idea of having him under my control. "Long enough. We're going back. Come."

He fights the order, but his feet move anyway, falling into step beside me. An owl screeches, making both of us tense and scan the area but we see nothing.

I slip an arm through his. "Did you ever seek revenge on anyone?"

He quirks his head at the question. "Before or after the change?"

"After."

"Avenging transgressions from my original human life?"

I nod. He carried me farther from the hospital than I'd thought. There are many blocks yet to go. Having him pick me up and race back might not be such a bad idea.

"Becoming a vampyre is a painful process, even more so than the blood cleansing. I spent months as a newborn, raging and unable to control my appetite. My human existence was inconsequential, even after I learned to control my hunger."

"Did your sire get what he wanted? Did your blood contain some type of unusual magical properties?"

"It does, but appears to be non-transferable. He gained none of my power."

"Your sire... he isn't around anymore, is he?"

I sense his smile. "Revenge can be satisfying."

The tone in his voice sends a shiver down my spine. "Remind me not to cross you." I eye the melting snow on the lawns and slushy streets. "Just how far did you take us?"

"Sixteen blocks."

"Sixteen?!"

"I fear too much sugar has caused your body to become weak. I will carry you the rest of the way."

I reach into my pocket to find a few cinnamons. Popping one in my mouth, I give him a dismissive snort. "I don't blame Izzy for wanting revenge. I did cause her death."

"How do you plan to stop her? Throw one of those horrible lemon drops in her mouth to make her do your bidding?"

If only it were that easy. I haven't existed this long without becoming adept at protecting myself. "No need to worry about me. I want you to create a distraction when we get back to the hospital."

"Why?"

He has never encountered a witch like Izzy before. "Our first concern is Betty. She seems to possess a link to my old friend now—possibly from that bite. Izzy was looking for a way to trap me and used Betty to do it. I believe Betty is fighting the coma and trying to tell me something. I just don't know what."

There has to be a way for me to reach her—the true friend I was once so close to. Some way to gain her trust and re-establish our friendship.

We fall silent until we reach the parking lot, me attempting to formulate a solid plan to get Izzy to reveal what she and Veramis are up to. "What is the signal?" Torren asks.

My magic scans the landscape, noting only a dull trail of shimmering dust gliding away from the southeast side of the building. "I don't believe we'll need one." I point to it. "She's gone."

A pulse of his Undead power radiates out from him like ripples in a pond. "But she's left a calling card." He sniffs the air.

He can smell it while I can see it. Interesting. There are times when we do make a good team. "Like breadcrumbs." We enter the clinic, and my blood turns cold at the amount of activity going on. Nurses and aides rush up and down the hall. Alarms are going off. "What's happened?" I demand from a passing nurse.

Fear coats her features. "Miss Betty," she says, a quiver in her voice.

"What about her?" Torren commands.

I can barely speak. "Is she...?" Torren takes my arm and squeezes.

"She's gone." The nurse glances up and down the hallway.

"Gone?" I echo, fearing the worst.

The nurse nods. "She removed her IV and the heart monitor. It appears she went out her window."

"How is that possible?" Torren asks. "She awoke from a coma and was able to jump out a window?"

I drag him toward the exit. "She didn't leave by her own accord."

The double glass door swooshes open, and we step out into the night.

He knows the answer, but he asks anyway. "Then how?"

I pop another cinnamon, eyeing the glistening dust trail leading south. "Izzy kidnapped her."

Chapter Sixteen

The dust taunts me like breadcrumbs through a forest—a blatant trap.

I'm ready to follow it, anyway, but Marlena intervenes. "Not so fast, Princess." She's waiting for us in the parking lot. Jo and Cyn are with her. Trinken, too. "You're going home."

"I need to follow Izzy and save Betty."

She's in her leathers, Gunther in hand. "First, I scout the location. Then we'll come up with a strategy."

"I have a strategy. I will trade myself for Betty and learn what Veramis and Izzy are up to so I can foil them."

"How will you escape their clutches if they don't kill you first?"

That's the part I haven't worked out yet. "I'll find a way. I'm not without resources."

"Yes," the mayor says. "You have us."

"Take her back to the shop," Marlena orders, and before I can argue, she muzzles me with a shot of mute magic. Not only does it seal my lips, it renders me immobile. While she and

Trinken leave to follow the trail, I am hauled to the candy shop and deposited in the back room.

My deepest desire is to save Betty and rectify the past. Waiting and doing nothing while my godmother risks herself nearly kills me. Even after the mute magic dissipates, my body-guards keep me locked in. They refuse to listen to my pleas or discuss the matter with me.

I pace until baking is the only outlet I have to ease my anxiety.

First, I mix up gingerbread for the houses and stick a tray in the oven. Then I work on cinnamon muffins.

Each time a freshly baked tray leaves the oven, a new pan goes in. I'm so focused on filling the front cases, my mind working through the Izzy situation, the displays are over-flowing when the dawn rises from its bed.

Izzy's face flashes in my mind's eye as I review our meeting at the portal. Something is off, yet I can't put my finger on it.

I replay the scene in my head— our arrival, then hers. The shadow elves. Her words, the rings on her fingers. Every detail plays out in slow motion while I wash bowls and clean up the kitchen.

My hands still. I see her reach out to stroke Cyn's arm. I see the flash of light on those rings. The blue sigil. My own words come back to me... *You're the closest thing I've ever had to a sister, and I love you.*

Then, without warning, I think of Torren. I hear his words next. *He threatened my sister. There is nothing I would not do for her.*

'Is.' He used the present tense.

Holy marshmallows. Is Torren's sister alive? A vampyre, too? How else could she have survived all this time?

Perhaps he simply misspoke.

Or perhaps he's pulling a layer of cotton candy over my eyes.

When Marlena returns, she changes clothes but keeps Gunther handy. She has sent Trinken on his way. Cyn, Torren, and Jo crowd in to hear her report. "I followed the dust to a farm northeast of town. Cute place, right out of a faerytale. Tons of flowers, a welcome sign even. There's a garden with a tiny waterfall behind the house."

"Misdirection," Torren says. "That acreage belongs to Cambria. It appears charming but hides many dark secrets."

She dons her apron and releases her curls from a hair band, shaking them out. "There were shadow elves skulking around, but not the numbers we witnessed at the portal. All of them seemed on edge, nervous, as if they expected Izzy to lash out at any moment."

"Or Veramis?" I ask.

"I didn't see or sense her, only Izzy. I know it's been a while since I was around your friend," Marlena continues, "but something seems...strange about her."

"I've been thinking the same." I pour her a cup of tea. "What about Betty?"

"I didn't see her, but there's a building that's heavily guarded on the east side."

"Could be where Izzy is keeping her," Jo says. "Is it a good spot for a trap?"

She sips the tea, a tightness leaving her shoulders. "Seems likely, but like I said, something isn't right about the whole thing."

"And there was no sign of Cambria?" Torren asks.

"None." She fishes in a pocket. "Found this, though."

It's a metal pin, a broach, one that makes my breath catch. I take it, a one-of-a-kind piece meant to adorn a royal cloak.

My fingers trail over the intricate crest causing the golden sun emblazoned in the center to light up at my touch.

Onyx warms, but not in a protective way. In a familiar, inviting way. "But this is..."

The implications of Izzy having this pin blow my mind. Such a thing never leaves the royal court, much less the kingdom. My mother would die before letting it out of her sight.

Marlena sees my shock and squeezes my arm. "I'm afraid we need to prepare for the worst."

I look at my godmother, my hand closing over the pin. "No. We just saw her in the portal. She's..." The sharp edges cut into my skin. "It can't be. She can't have taken my mother too."

The others exchanged an alarmed glance. "That's your mother's?" Torren asks.

I nod, biting my bottom lip to keep a tear from escaping my eye.

Marlena sets down her cup. "Contact the realm and assure us that the queen is safe."

The pin grows hot like a fire in my hand. "She's alive and well," I insist.

Marlena puts an arm around my shoulders, pretending not to see the tears limning my eyes. "I pray it's true, Princess, but if not, we will need to make plans."

She squeezes my shoulders, and I raise my gaze. "You know I can't do that..."

Her eyes are steady and calm. "You may have no choice in the matter. If the Queen is dead, your father will be devastated and unable to lead. The fate of Ever After will fall to you. You must take up the cloak."

Chapter Seventeen

There's a lot to be said for living in an enchanted realm. I have missed the beauty and the most peaceful of days.

The ache in my chest, however, isn't for the past life I had there. I realize now that it is from my parents exiling me to this place. At the time, it seemed like a betrayal that they could think the worst of me and make me an *Outcast*. Now, I know here is where I belong.

My goals shift to encompass the Queen: Save Mother. Rescue Betty. Stop Izzy. Uncover the truth about Torren and his sister. About Nightbane.

I'm not sure there's enough candy in any of the realms to help me with all of it. But Jo is right—I have resources.

Marlena and I have devised a master plan to rival anything the Black Heart Court has ever seen.

I send a raven to Trinken this time, requesting a meeting of any and all *Outcasts* to assemble. I have to deal with Izzy one-on-one, but having an enchanted army at my back will help.

At twilight, just as the Reindeer Scavenger Hunt is kicking off, I step out back and open up to my Ever After magic.

It's the first time I've fully released it and let it rise since being banished here. If any non-magicals witnessed it, they might not live to tell the tale.

When I came through the portal, my skin and hair lost their color, and I also lost my magic for a while. Now, it fills me up, and although my previous tan skin and red hair do not return, I sparkle as the magic sighs with relief at being released.

Elementals begin to step forth from behind trees and bushes—faeries, pixies, gnomes, and more. Trinken, in goblin form, appears beside my oak tree, his hand clasping his wife's.

Hookba smiles and drops a curtsy. Others follow. As one, they soak in my royal power with bowed heads, murmuring blessings on me.

"Do not put yourselves beneath me or any other being tonight," I say, moving through the group and lifting those on their knees to their feet. I hail you only to seek your assistance."

Marlena joins us, Gunther in hand. She idles in the doorway, scanning the meager assembly.

"Why?" a faery asks. She appears short, round, and aged. A fat dog wiggles in her arms—a protective glamour.

"There is danger afoot for all of us." I brief them on what has occurred, including my suspicions. I lift the royal pin, and it shimmers with power. A unified '*ohhh*' echoes through the group.

The faery sheds her glamour, becoming petite, her skin sparkling pink, her hair a rainbow. The dog becomes a small unicorn, standing beside her. "The Queen is here? In the land of the Barren?"

"There are no reports of her missing from the realm," Trinken states. "But she has not been seen since our meeting in the fringe."

Marlena leans against the doorframe. "The King would

keep her disappearance quiet for as long as possible. With her missing and the Crown Princess exiled, the kingdom could fall to chaos."

Murmurs ripple through the crowd. A gnome steps forward. "I'm Glidon," he says. "With due respect, I have no love for your mother. While you've been kind to us, we ended up here because of her."

He ended up here because he broke the rules. Or perhaps, like me, he was misjudged. I offer compassion. "I appreciate your candidness. You were exiled for crimes against the crown, and the king and queen are duty-bound to uphold the laws. No one here is on trial, and if you were wrongly accused, I will see to it that the wrong is righted." A tall order, but I mean it. "Whether we agree or disagree with our punishments, I ask that you consider what may happen if Ever After falls. The Black Heart Court will take over this realm and our former one. Veramis will place bounties on the heads of all Outcasts or force us into submission to carry out her whims."

Marlena twirls Gunther. "Most of us have found refuge and peace here and wish to continue our lives among the Barren. If Izzy and her mother succeed, that will no longer be an option. For those of you waiting out your sentence in order to return to our magical home, I assure you there will be no home to return to."

The echo of our words hangs in the air. In the distance, I hear children's laughter. If we fail tonight, they will never again celebrate Christmas.

Trinken steps to my side. He looks out over those gathered. "I follow the princess."

A spattering of others joins him, each stating their oath. "I follow the princess."

A few disappear, fading into the shadows. I silently wish

them well on their quests, even though I am disappointed. Glidon surprises me and stays.

I meet the eye of each who stands with me, my stomach filled with acidic butterflies. "I won't ask you to follow me without telling you my agenda. I want you to make an informed decision before you commit."

"Hello...?"

Before I can call my magic back, Maude appears, pushing past a dormant camellia bush. "There you are."

I throw up a screen so the enchanted are hidden as her voice fades off at the sight of Trinken. Marlena rushes forward, blocking her view. "What are you doing here?"

Trinken slips behind my veil. I turn my back to Maude, now distracted by Marlena. I draw my magic inside like sucking a milkshake through a straw. The rushed reversal leaves me lightheaded.

"I came to see why the shop is closed," the dentist says. "The kids are lined up out front."

I face her with a smile. "Maude, I'm glad you're here."

"You are?" she and Marlena ask in unison.

I usher the woman inside, giving my godmother a quick *be quiet* glance. "Yes, I need someone to hand out the treat bags for me." I forgot to make them up, but with a wave of my hand, a tray of them appear, festive bows complete with tiny bells.

I so love magic. I just hope I haven't overdone it.

"Marlena and I will be gone an hour or so. Can you handle it?"

She looks as if I've suggested she jump off a high bridge. "You want me to hand out candy."

"It's all-natural and won't rot anyone's teeth. I promise." I drag her to the front of the shop. "We would really appreciate it. We have a...family emergency to take care of."

Before I can escape, she grabs my arm. "Are you in some kind of trouble?"

Boy, am I. The children outside call through the glass to me, waving with mittened hands. They jump up and down when I wave back. "No, of course not. I wouldn't miss a single minute of this if I didn't have to. Please, Maude. I promise to return the favor."

That makes her squeeze my arm. "You must really be in a pickle."

"I am."

Her frown lingers, but she nods. "Go then, I'll take care of the kids."

I give her a return squeeze. "I knew I could count on you."

"What about the others?"

Did she see the creatures in the garden? "Others?"

"We're here," Torren says. He, Cyn, and Jo, have come in the back door.

"Oh, plum cakes," I mutter under my breath.

Cyn grins. "You didn't think we'd let you go without us, did you?"

Maude pushes me toward them. "Take care of your family emergency...and whatever else you need to do to help Betty."

"You know about Betty?"

Jo tugs me with him to the back exit. "Maude knows a lot more than she lets on."

"We're wasting time," Torren says, as the trio shove me out into the night. Malena laughs, ready for action.

Chapter Eighteen

Cambria's farm is somewhat disappointing. I expected more of a compound, a gothic castle, or at least a stately Victorian two-story. What I see as we approach the generous acreage surrounded by ancient oaks is exactly like my godmother described—a faerytale.

The two-story house with an attic is ghastly white under the moon, with bougainvillea vines and ivy climbing a turret on one side. A display with Santa's sleigh and brightly wrapped presents sits on the porch.

A stone walk rambles around the side, solar lights in the shape of night-blooming flowers with deep throats and glistening petals lighting the path.

The cedar shakes appear like frosted gingerbread. A smattering of other trees and bushes, along with a garden in the back—still flourishing, no doubt due to magic—create a homey atmosphere.

Fingers of frost snake across the lawn, though, and the porch light spotlighting the welcome sign on the door gives off repelling vibes.

On closer inspection, I note signs of witchcraft. Nightshade and asafetida line the undead garden. A pentagram, invisible to non-magicals, marks the barn's wooden doors, and a witch's bell hangs on both the front and rear entrances. Nothing overt that the general public would suspect, but clear signs to those that practice the craft.

I pop a candy toadstool. "I expected a big bad witch who heads an extremely powerful coven would have a more..."

"Scarier place?" Cyn finishes.

I see a ripple in the landscape and allow my magic to hone in on it. My eyes see through the scene in front of me. Now things make more sense. "Illusion magic. She's glamoured the place so mundanes don't bother her."

"Where are the elves?" Jo asks, scanning the landscape.

Marlena sticks close to him. "They're here, just out of sight. Keep an eye out for anything that seems odd."

"Odder than a bunch of faerytale characters, a vampyre, a renegade shifter, and a fallen angel?" Jo quips, glancing over his shoulder at our army.

My ragtag group has been joined by some of Torren's Undead. While they appear invisible, I can sense them. His army seems to be younger than he is and eager for battle.

I infuse my vocal cords with amplifier magic so everyone can pick up my thoughts telepathically. *"Your only job is to rescue the human Betty and any other being held against their will."* I finger the royal crest in my pocket. *"Leave Izzy and her mother to me."* I send an image of both from my mind to theirs.

Silent confirmations fill my head. I make eye contact with the three males next to me, switching back to normal and keeping my voice low. "Whatever happens, do not try to interfere or rescue me. I want promises from each of you. You're to cover the others and make sure they get out safe. Swear to it."

None of them like this bargain, but they do as requested. Torren's eyes are lit with something I can't decipher, but even he gives me his vow.

I face the open yard, a single light on a tall pole near the barn joins the moon in illuminating the lawn. "It will take all of my magic to fight her," I tell them. "Izzy is my equal in most ways. If it was only her and I, I have no doubt I would win. If her mother is here, however, things will get dicey. Trust in me. I have a backup that can stop them both."

Cyn points to Marlena. "Her?"

I pull the gargoyle from around my neck, tossing the amulet on the ground at my feet. "Whatever happens, please know I have very much enjoyed being friends with each of you."

"Seraphina...Princess." Torren moves toward me, but Marlena stops him.

"Better step back, bloodsucker." The pendant pops and hisses, and he jumps. The vampyre's self-preservation is strong.

Onyx clearly does not belong in this world, his scales and beastly face frightening to most everyone, even in Ever After. All eyes watch as he grows from an inch in size to a giant.

Gunther, still in Marlena's hands, cries, *"Not fair. I want off my leash, too!"*

I ignore the saucer-shaped eyes of my friends glued to the menacing gargoyle towering over them. Onyx scoops up a paw of snow and eats it.

"Let's go," I say to him and my godmother.

Striding across the open yard, Onyx's heavy footsteps thudding behind me, I call out to my former friend and now enemy. "Izzy, show yourself!"

All is unnaturally silent as if someone has turned off the volume. I sense Cyn, Torren, and Jo, aligning our troops, ready to rush the building to find Betty and possibly my mother. Trinken and his soldiers stay hidden, an invisible force for our flanks should we need a second wave.

The wait feels too long. My magic screams, impatient. With my muscles tense and my mind uneasy, I anticipate the coming fight, yet when no one comes for me, I begin to wonder if Izzy or Veramis are here.

A sideways glance at Marlena shows me her pivoting in a slow circle. Gunther continues to complain. Onyx huffs, white clouds forming around his muzzle.

"Where is she?" Marlena murmurs.

The *Outcasts* with us are on edge. Their anxious energy zips over my skin. In my head, I hear their thoughts like dozens of bees in a hive.

"I may have to go in after her," I tell them. *"You will stay here."*

I lift a hand to signal Torren to advance on the barn, but movement on the porch stops me.

Izzy materializes. Her lips are black in the moonlight, and she licks them. "Look what Santa brought me—a royal princess of faerytale fame. I've been waiting for you."

Chapter Nineteen

She doesn't even glance at my guardian, my godmother, or the *Outcasts*. Her gaze is fixated on me and only me.

I hold my ground, suspecting she might be nothing but a distraction. I send a mental order for Trinken and the others to be on alert for an ambush. "Hello, my friend."

She snickers. "You're no friend of mine. Not anymore"

"Remember the cherry twists I used to make for you? You ate them by the bucket. That one time, right before the summer solstice, you got so sick!" I sigh at the funny memory. "I thought your mother would kill us both."

My attempt at jogging her memory seems to confuse her. "What?"

Elves emerge from a variety of hiding spots, forming a circle around those of us on the front lawn. Their power lies in their numbers, and they are cautious of Onyx, who can squash a dozen of them with one step.

Marlena positions her back to mine while the gargoyle growls and chuffs under his breath. His shadow falls protectively over us.

"I miss you," I tell Izzy. "I know you have no love for me right now, but I want to apologize. I don't know what happened that day. All I know is that things aren't what they seem, then or now."

Her left eye twitches. An emerald necklace on her collarbone flickers, catching the moonlight.

Emerald—she always preferred rubies, the same color as her favorite flavor—cherry.

My attention falls on her rings, a stack of bracelets, and the decorative buttons on the elaborately stitched wool coat she wears. The ornamentation isn't like her. Is it possible she embraced different things after her resurrection?

"Is there any way we can come to an agreement?" I ask. "A way for us to both get what we want?"

She tilts her head, and a tendon pops. Her eyes finally focus on Onyx, then lower to meet mine. "The only agreement that interests me involves the vampyre."

"What do you want with Torren?"

The eye twitches again. "Not your pet," she snarls. Her voice takes on an unusual undertone. "The one of the prophecy."

Nightbane? "I can't offer him, but you can have me if you free Betty."

Another pop of her neck and her chin jerks to the right as if being pulled by a string. "Oh, I'll have you, but I want the ultimate weapon."

Considering that with her powers, she should technically be a weapon herself, I find that statement ironic. A sliver of black magic slithers over my shield. Is she attempting to distract me so her mother can incapacitate me in some way?

I need to turn the tables on her. "I don't remember you

being so dramatic. Nor would you need Nightbane if you were truly the Crown Princess of the Black Heart Court."

Her gaze darts to Onyx once more. "You have your beast. Why can't I have mine?"

Onyx growls low, and I feel his energy rising. "Only for protection. Never to harm."

"Call him off." Her voice climbs several octaves. "You work for me now."

I jut my chin toward the closest elves. "Call off yours first."

Her face twitches, and her head jerks, the tendrils of black magic clawing against my shield now.

The opaque apparition of a second head appears and disappears in a blur. I blink, believing my vision is wonky.

On the porch, a true ghost appears—Flower. "Hey," she calls, waving to me. As always, she's dressed for summer in bell bottoms and a tank top. "Did you know she's possessed?"

Eyes glittering, Izzy shudders, then seems to collect herself. She seems blind to Flower, which works in my favor. She grits her teeth as she speaks. "Bring me the ancient one of the prophecy, and I'll spare you."

She has no intention of sparing me, and one question is on reply in my head—why does she want Nightbane?

A new voice shoves itself into my swirling thoughts. *"Help me!"*

"Possessed," Flower calls, sitting on Santa's sleigh.

"What do I do?" I ask the ghost. I've never dealt with such a thing.

It's as if two heads top Izzy's body now, and she thinks I'm talking to her. "You heard me!" Her voice thunders across the lawn. "Bring me the Undead's Chosen One. Only then will I return Betty."

Flower is rattling on about possession and priests. "Oh, that's right! You have the Rev with you! I bet he could perform an exorcism." An owl hoots, and she glances up at it where it perches on a tree branch. "Hello, little owl. Do you know Santa?"

Even in death, she is like a child, easily distracted.

The other voice in my head comes through again. It is urgent, scared. *"Help me, Ambrosia."* My eyes snap to Izzy's face—two faces. I know that voice. It can't be— or can it? *"Candy drop."*

I haven't heard that code since Izzy and I were eleven. We devised a sting operation to steal enchanted marshmallows from the kingdom's kitchen to feed a family of hedgehogs in the forest we wished to keep as pets.

"Candy drop," I reply in acknowledgment.

Marlena nudges me. "What's going on?"

I snap out of the memory of the cook catching us and my father demanding we reveal our intentions. I'd lied and told him it was for the candy cottage I was building, which my parents didn't know about at the time. My father was delighted at our ingenuity, but my mother and Veramis suspected there was more to it.

We were later caught with our magically drugged pets, and disciplined. The unwilling hedgehogs were released back to their home. While Izzy and I disliked the chores and restrictions placed on our freedom as punishment, we were undaunted. Our next Candy Drop Operation involved bears... not to make them pets, but to hide a mother and cubs who had wandered into the fringe and become stuck.

Candy Drop became our code for many things—a warning for when our parents were approaching, a request for help, a statement of solidarity.

I step toward the Izzy look-alike. "What's the only candy I detest?"

Her brows lower, her body shudders, her fingers twitch. "What?"

"You heard me."

Magic crackles at the end of her fingertips. She walks down the steps and into the yard. "Stop playing games."

I inch closer, moving toward her and hoping to draw her attention, and that of her elves, away from the barn. "Is your memory faulty, Izzy? Did death blot it out?"

Marlena and Onyx move alongside me, following my cue. The elves shift, adjusting their ring. Out of the corner of my eye, I see a faint ripple near the barn's entrance. Torren and his team are planting the candies I supplied in a ring around the building.

They look like gummy worms, and like real ones who eat soil, these will eat through wards. Placed in the four cardinal directions, they can disable any and all magic within the circumference.

"What are you up to?" she demands as I continue to the house.

"If we're going to discuss strategy regarding the capture of Nightbane, I prefer to do it inside. A hot cup of tea would be nice."

"Stop!" I see her visibly shaking, red-hot energy shooting from her fingers into the ground. The laser beams melt the snow, causing steam to rise. The emerald at her collarbone pulses. "You're not going anywhere."

The temperature drops. I point at the holes she's created in the ground. "Funny, but I don't recall my Izzy ever having powers over the elements."

In this realm, however, many witches do.

Cambria. Possession.

It all becomes clear.

"I remember the summer we attempted to make elderberry wine and nearly poisoned ourselves."

Her face shifts and morphs through multiple responses, as if she can't control her features. "Enough of the stroll down memory lane. If you want Betty, bring me—"

"It was apple wine," I interrupt. "And I detest licorice."

Realizing I know the truth, Cambria lifts Izzy's hands and shoots a set of those red laser beams right at my chest.

Chapter Twenty

Several things happen at once: Marlena hollers. Onyx bellows. I throw my magic out in a shield.

It doesn't simply protect us; it reflects the beams back at her.

Cambria isn't able to dodge both, and one strikes her in the shoulder, burning through the fabric of her coat and into her skin. The force knocks her off her feet.

She jumps up, glancing at her wound. "You..." she sputters and staggers. "I'll kill you!"

The hologram-like head tries to pull itself free. The face contorts, then disappears.

But Izzy—*my* Izzy—doesn't stop fighting. Cambria's glamour fades, and she staggers, a war going on inside the body between the two of them.

This is my chance to incapacitate her. From my cape, I draw out red licorice strings and toss them at her feet. "Take her down," I command.

They come to life, wiggling and growing and becoming as

large as anacondas. She screams, and the elves rush me, but the candy does its job, entangling her feet and causing her to fall.

Marlena and Gunther fight the elves.

Onyx roars, the sound shaking the ground.

"Lock," I shout to the licorice snakes. They clamp together on one end and wrap around her ankles.

I toss aside elves who get in my way as I charge her. I hear shouts from the barn and know the wards have fallen. "Reverend!" I yell.

Trinken and his army join me and Marlena, descending on the elves. I hear Cyn reply, but he is surrounded by more elves and can't get to us.

Cambria kicks at the licorice, trying to use magic to dislodge it. She tries to crawl away, all the while sputtering and muttering spells.

I withdraw a dozen of my gummy bears, whispering over them. "Choke and bind."

They wing from my hand into her mouth as she speaks. She coughs and tries to spit them out.

Onyx howls in pain, the noise sending a shiver down my spine. I glance back to see elves stabbing him with all manner of weapons—axes, blades, hammers. One has managed to get on his back, and another rides on one of his legs.

"Seraphina! Watch out!" Torren's cry turns my attention back to Cambria, the crackly red magic forming at her fingertips. She flings it at me, and as I raise a hand to block it, a blur of a figure passes between us.

Torren.

As the lasers hit, it's his body that absorbs them. He crumples at my feet, silent and still.

Too still, even for him.

Anger rages through me as fierce and uncontrollable as a

wildfire. The fuzzy memory of Izzy attacking Gretel merges with the sight of a lifeless Torren. He is burned and sizzling where the beams have seared through his clothes, his skin.

The elves close in like a swarm of bees. Another howl goes up from Onyx. I can't see Marlena. The clash of blades rings in the night, as do cries of triumph and defeat.

I'm down to nothing but lemon drops, but I send one to Torren, the candy floating into his slack mouth. "Don't die," I command, stepping over him to bear down on Cambria.

She crawls toward the porch, but her body is fighting her—or, I should say, Izzy is. I grab her by the hair and pull her head back, exposing her neck and forcing her mouth open. I deposit a lemon drop, causing her eyes to bug out. "Be still."

Her body goes rigid. I stare into her eyes, releasing her hair, and forcing her onto her back. "Any entity not Izzy, show yourself."

The second head appears to the left of the original, a ghostly face that peels away. Flower gasps and claps.

In one fluid movement, Cambria's spirit detaches completely, hesitating for a split second. Before I can freeze it, it evaporates.

The elves stop and look around, blinking in confusion as Cambria's magic hold on them dissipates.

"Lower your weapons," Trinken commands from the center of the yard.

The elves wisely do so, their movements sluggish.

Onyx extracts several blades stuck in his rough hide. He drops them like needles to the ground, then swipes at a couple of the culprits who injured him, sending the elves flying.

Jo and Cyn rush to Torren. Marlena, limping, closes the distance, staring down at the now-immobile Izzy. "I'm confused. What in the name of faerytales just happened?"

"Cambria possessed Izzy's body, but it's unclear how Izzy is alive." I glance at Jo. "Did you rescue Betty?"

He nods. "There wasn't anyone else, though."

I'm both relieved and disappointed. Until I can confirm the Queen is missing, however, there's nothing else I can do. "Is she okay?"

"Shook up, but she's talking and seems like her usual self."

That brings relief. Torren's unmoving body does not. I drop to my knees and shake him. "Stupid vampyre! What did I tell you? I don't need or want rescuing!"

Marlena tugs me away and drags me to Izzy. My brain is already turning over ideas about how to resurrect Torren, but I stop myself—necromancy? No way.

But is it necromancy if he's already dead?

"What about her?" Marlena asks, the tip of Gunther hovering over Izzy's throat.

"Speak," I command. My energy is swiftly leaving. "Who are you?"

Her closed eyes open, and they are filled with tears. "Ambrosia?"

There's something in her gaze that wasn't there before. My heart soars. "Who was the first boy you kissed?"

Her lips tremble in a faint smile. "Culavan Hardbroom."

A deep satisfaction washes through me, replacing my doubt. "It's indeed you."

"I was trying to push her out—that witch. Trying to reach you, to let you know I wasn't doing all those things."

"How did she possess you?"

Izzy sits up, grabbing the emerald at her neck. She yanks it, breaking the chain, and throws it into the snow. "That stone is charmed. It allowed her to use my body."

I scan the night, wondering where Cambria is now. "And hers? Is it in the house?"

"There's a hidden room below ground with a witch's circle. The body's inside that."

"I'm on it," Marlena says, hobbling for the house. Gunther hoots with anticipation.

Jo runs after them. "I'll go with her."

"I don't understand what's happened." Izzy brings a shaky hand to her face, rubbing it across her forehead. "Where are we? Why am I here?"

Trinken and the *Outcasts* have gathered around us. They whisper behind their hands and point. Torren's vampyres are gathered around his body, blocking him from my view.

"What's the last thing you remember?" I ask.

She stares at her lap. "Your cabin. I was coming to see you and bring you a batch of sugar plums. I—" Her forehead creases, her eyes meet mine. "Things are a blank after that."

She doesn't remember the fight. Dying.

I remove the pin from my pocket. "My mother—do you know if Cambria kidnapped her?"

Izzy rears back. She points at it. "She used that in the spell."

"She used this to possess you?" At her nod, I turn the pin over and over, thinking. "You don't know how she acquired it?"

A shake of her head.

"How is that possible?" I mumble to myself, and those around me shake their head in answer. I feel Trinken's heavy gaze, and I peek at him, seeing my fear reflected in his face.

The most obvious explanation is the least palpable—the Queen gave it to her.

Marlena emerges from the house with Jo. "The body is in stasis. What do you want to do?"

I slip the pin into my cape and retrieve the necklace from the snowbank. "Spread out, hunt down Cambria's ghost. We can't allow her to possess anyone else, and we must uncover the truth about how she came into control of this pin."

They do as commanded, and I release the licorice ties around Izzy's feet. They scatter, and I help her stand. "Wait here, okay?"

The vampyres part for me and I crouch next to Torren once more. Cyn is on the other side, praying over him.

"Why did he do that?" I ask on a sob.

His folded hands clench and unclench. "He cares—cared —about you."

Onyx lowers his muzzle and sniffs the body. He gives it a nudge with his nose. Drool drips from his mouth, splashing on Torren's cheek.

My heart does funny acrobatics in my chest. My eyes tear from the cold air—at least that's what I tell myself—and my nose is clogged. I grab him by his broad shoulders and shake him hard. "I commanded you not to die!"

I'm still shaking him when his hands suddenly grab mine, and his eyes flip open. "I dislike lemon," he says, "as much as I hate taking orders."

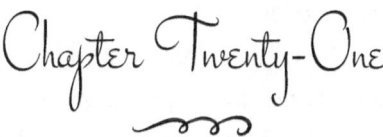

Chapter Twenty-One

We return to town bedraggled but alive and just in time for the last hour of the Reindeer Scavenger Hunt. Maude is immensely relieved to see me, the night filled with children and sugar.

"Thanks for your help." I direct her to the shop door. "I take it all went well?"

She gently shakes off my hand from her arm and peeks at Izzy over my shoulder. "Busy as a beaver. I've never had this many kids come to my clinic for treats."

Because you hand out toothbrushes. "I'll take over now. Thanks again."

"Is that the witch from the other night?" Maude struggles to keep looking back.

"She's the family emergency, and the role-playing is over," I assure her. "She's decided to be a good witch." I wink as if this is part of the game.

Kids pack the shop, making us shift this way and that as I coax her toward the exit. Many of them hug me around the waist and show off their collections of items from the hunt. The excitement of Christmas fills the shop, and I hear the familiar laughter of our resident ghost boy—he's loving it, too. He's been quiet for so long, I wondered if he'd moved on.

Out of sight of the crowd, Marlena remakes her clothing with a sweep of her hand and hustles to the front to take care of the children. She hands out the last of the treats. Afraid they might not get one, the kids cluster around her.

Both the emerald and the royal pin are in my pocket. I coax Maude outside. "I hear Betty is awake," I tell her. "Looks like she's going to be fine."

"Oh, that's good to hear. Is she home?"

A few of the children race from the shop, calling, "Merry Christmas!"

I raise a hand and return the sentiment. On the way back, Torren gently wiped Betty's mind of any thoughts associated with Cambria and Izzy, and Jo assisted her to the clinic for a check-up.

From what I could see, she was her usual, feisty self. I told her she'd had a funny reaction to my strawberries, which had landed her in the hospital. Jo elaborated on the story, explaining how, at some point, she had wandered off, and luckily, we'd been able to find her.

She seemed to believe most of it, although disappointment was evident over the strawberries. "I've never had any kind of allergic reaction to them before," she'd insisted.

"And you likely never will again," I'd reassured her.

"She's staying one more night at the clinic," I tell Maude. The sky has cleared, and stars twinkle overhead. "We plan to visit first thing in the morning, and Jo will take her home once the doctor releases her."

"Well, that's great." Maude continues to stare into the shop. "What a crazy week, huh?"

"Are you ready for Christmas?"

"I, uh...sure." She shrugs, a touch of sadness in her face. "I'm not much on celebrations."

Flower appears, staring up at the stars. "Because she's alone. Holidays are tough when you don't have anyone to share them with."

A young girl in an elf costume hugs me, her mother waiting on the sidewalk. We exchange wishes for a happy holiday, and they move on.

"Maybe you just need a new tradition." I wink at Maude. "Would you like to come over Christmas morning for tea?"

Her face brightens. "You would do that? Share your holiday with me?"

Marlena will kill me, or at least grumble endlessly about it, but I have an idea. "Of course. We're all family here, right? See you at nine?"

She nods, a smile on her face, as she toddles off to her place.

We close up, and Torren, Cyn, Marlena, and I polish off the meager leftovers of the day. Izzy accepts a warm cup of cocoa but is exhausted, so I tuck her into my bed upstairs. "I'm so confused," she says, yawning.

"You and me both, but we'll figure it out."

She falls asleep and I smooth a dark strand of hair from her cheek. Tomorrow, I'll create a spell to restore her memories. In Ever After, none are needed—we don't forget. Yet, I can't remember exactly what happened that night at my cabin. I only have the replay of what was shown at my trial, and I have more questions than answers from that. In this realm, there are witches who practice many types of the craft, and surely one of them might be able to help us.

Meantime, I'll cast my own divination to locate my mother.

"Trinken's here," Marlena whispers from the doorway. "He's brought the ghost."

We gather in the backyard. Hookah carries the spirit in an iron and glass container. The female goblin dips into a curtsy and holds it out to me. "Your Highness."

"The evil witch is not talking," Trinken says.

Cambria's spirit snarls through the glass as I examine her. "You will when I'm done with you."

Torren takes the jar from me. "Jo is trying to figure out how we can return her to her body. My vampyres are guarding the farmhouse and will make sure the body remains in stasis until that time. They will also repel any who drop by. Meanwhile, I'll handle her interrogation and any justice the council feels appropriate when the time comes. You have a reputation to uphold, after all." It's said with a hint of teasing.

While I'm reluctant to turn over the spirit, it's for the best. "Yes, well, I would like to be kept in the loop. It was my friend she used for her purposes, and I don't take that lightly."

He inclines his head. "As you wish."

My relief at his resurrection surfaces again as I stare into his eyes. His power ripples through the air, warming me. A weighted silence falls between us, the others watching in fascination.

Queen.

The single word echoes in my head, and if I didn't know better, I'd swear he put it there.

Flower pops into view, leaning on a tree. "He's dreamy," she says with awe in her voice.

He is that. Like smooth gelato melting on my tongue.

Marlena clears her throat. Torren's grin tells me he knows exactly where my mind went.

Shaking it off, I address those crowding my property. "Your

assistance tonight will be repaid. If you need my aid for anything, let me know."

Glidon steps forward. "And your mother?"

I touch the pin inside my pocket. "I'm working on that."

Trinken is tracking Veramis, who he's discovered is missing from Ever After. Marlena wants to help him, but she has more Outcasts to transport before Christmas Day.

"Will you go home?" the faery from earlier asks.

What she really wants to know is if I'll be leaving them, or if I do return to Ever After, if I'll renounce their sentences.

Torren and others watch me carefully. The idea of abandoning all of them forms a hard pit in my stomach. "Only to visit." I smile. "This is my home now."

Chapter Twenty-Two

I always wanted a sister.

The next day, Izzy and I reminisce, and she samples every candy and pastry in the shop. Every few minutes, her face goes blank, and she stumbles over words. It's as if she's not all here.

Time, I assure myself. *She just needs time.* Since she's been through so much, I decide not to share the facts about her supposed death, my exile, and my ongoing suspicions about what her mother is up to until she regains her strength. Maybe she'll regain her memory, too.

I have to come up with a reason why we are both in the human world and not the enchanted realm, but she's so fascinated with this one that she doesn't question me when I explain I'm simply on the outs with my mother. "What's new?" she asks with a weak smile. She doesn't even ask about Veritas.

I send Marlena to take the mayor his morning turnover, and she discovers that Betty is back to work and asking for details about my gingerbread houses for the booth. Her sister is nearly her double, Marlena says, except for the pentagram necklace around her neck and the scent of patchouli she radiates.

At noon, Izzy retreats to bed, already worn out. Marlena takes over the front counter so I can concentrate on making ginger candies and peppermint gumdrops to use on the houses. She's tired, too, and neither of us feels like washing trays or answering the phone.

Petrina comes in and does both. Then she cuts out pieces of gingerbread according to my patterns. Her presence keeps us from discussing Izzy and my mother, but the distraction is welcome nonetheless.

Trinken leaves a message on the back steps under a potted holly plant. It bears the royal crest and my father's handwriting. Once I break the seal, the note reads itself in his familiar baritone. *Your mother is safe and well. Come home, Ambrosia. I miss you.*

A tear slides down my cheek. "I miss you, too, Dad."

After Petrina leaves at closing time, I hand the note to Marlena. Her brow furrows. "If she is safe and well, why did *he* send a note and not her?"

I shrug. "She probably ordered him to do it."

"Hmm. Maybe."

"What are you thinking?"

She hands the note back. "He says she's safe and well, but he doesn't say she's home, and we've received no official pardon regarding your exile."

"You're reading too much into it. She probably went to her palace in the mountains, not realizing she threw the kingdom and us into a small panic about her absence."

"We have no explanation for how her pin fell into Cambria's hands."

"And that mystery will eat at me until I uncover the truth, but we have a holiday to celebrate."

She makes a noncommittal noise and eyes the six ginger-bread houses—castles, really— that Petrina and I have built. "They're beautiful."

They are, and I'm proud of them. "What time do I have to be at the fair?"

"The doors open at two and it runs until six. Cyn already volunteered to help us transport them." She removes her apron and hangs it up. "If you don't need me for a few hours, I have some shopping to do."

"That shopping wouldn't happen to be for a certain angelic mayor, would it?"

She snags one of the leftover gingerbread scraps. "That, Your Highness, is none of your business."

After she's gone, I leave the ward open at the back door. As hoped, Torren appears shortly before midnight. He material-izes at my workstation, snagging a peppermint. "These are much more palatable than those atrocious lemon drops."

"Those lemon drops saved your life."

His gaze is steady and intense, making certain parts of my anatomy fire up like I have just rubbed peppermint oil on them. "*You* saved my life."

Onyx heats, but I know I'm not in danger. "I don't need a bodyguard. I'm more powerful than you."

He keeps up the eye contact as if daring me to look away. "So you say. Perhaps you would have survived Cambria's magic, but what if you hadn't? As you claim, you're the most magical person around, but if her lasers had brought your death or even severe injury, who here could heal you? Bring you back from death's clutches?"

There's a challenge in those words. "You think you could turn me into a vampyre?"

"To save your life, I am burdened to try. Think of it as first aid."

I laugh. "Well, let's hope it never comes to that."

He places a hand over his heart as if I have wounded him. "I'm disappointed you detest the idea so much."

Originally, I assumed he was trying to get me to be his queen because he craved my blood, and the fact he couldn't quite put his finger on what I was. Now he knows what I am, and he's still trying. Maybe it will make him even more determined. I find I look forward to the challenge. "I'm a sugar addict. I'd rather die than give it up."

He pops another candy into his mouth and considers my statement as he steps toward me. "There's no need to give up your indulgence."

They're only words, but the exchange feels like a seduction. My skin continues to tingle, his magic tickling it, while my heart races from his mesmerizing eyes. I step back. "The Undead don't need my services now that the assassin is no longer a threat."

Slow and easy, he glides closer, invading my personal space. "Kaine sends his regards. I'm quite sure we may call on you and your unique skills again."

I attempt to regain my composure and break from the pulsing energy between us. Another step back, even as I lick my lips. "I'm not for hire."

He leans a hip on the table, smiling. "Think of it as doing us a favor. In return—"

"No. No favors, no bargains, no contracts."

He chuckles. "As you wish."

Heat flares in my cheeks. I'm still curious about who he

was trying to protect, but I have a pretty good idea. "Night-bane means a great deal to you personally, doesn't she? That's why you came to me with all of this."

The seduction in his eyes cools. "I requested your assistance because I know your magic is different than mine. Between the two of us, we can, and did, create an unstoppable force, eliminating Cambria's threat."

"We had help." Onyx warms my skin as if appreciating the acknowledgment. "And Cambria killed you, as I recall."

He doesn't falter. "Not even close. My regenerative powers are unique among all creatures, possibly even those from your realm. The Undead nation will handle her."

"It's not that simple, Torren. She messed with one of mine. I was accused of murdering Izzy. Then she turns up here, possessed by a witch. It's a sensitive matter, with truths yet to be revealed."

"I'm quite adept at taking care of sensitive supernatural matters, and I'll assist you in unraveling the mystery behind all of it."

He's so sure of himself. Skirting the edge of the table, I work at cleaning up the mess I've made. "Sensitive ones like your sister?"

The cockiness turns to surprise. "You know."

A statement, not a question. "I guessed. Your protectiveness, the story you told me about her, and the way you were reluctant to fill me on why Nightbane was so important to the Undead Nation all suggested as such." I scrub a bowl and set it in the drainer, giving him time to say something or leave. He does neither. "How did it happen?" I ask. "How did she become this mythical creature?"

Turning away, he heads for the exit. I feel my stomach drop.

Then he stops and lowers his head. "The Angel of Death."

What? "Not the answer I was expecting." I dry my hands and lean against the counter. "How could an angel create such a being?"

His chest expands and deflates. "Utsas, my sire, fell in love with her. He wanted to bond with her. I would not allow it, but I knew it was only a matter of time."

Pivoting slowly on his expensive loafers, he faces me. "I stole a feather from the angel. I made her carry it with her at all times. I told her when Ustas came for her, to use it against him."

"You thought it would keep her human. Even if he tried to change her."

"The Undead stories claimed as much."

There's a 'but' in there somewhere. "Obviously, something backfired."

He stares at me, silent. "Yes."

I gesture for him to continue, but he simply stares at me, unwilling.

So stubborn. "Look, my mother commanded me to help you stop Cambria, so she knows about your sister and yet seems to have no qualms about your nation taking over the world by using her. On the other hand, somehow, the Queen's royal pin, an extremely powerful magical artifact, ended up in Cambria's hands. My friend has been returned from the dead, and Cambria possessed her to assassinate your sister." Saying it out loud, even after living through it, makes my head spin. "How did Cambria know about Izzy, and why her? Was my mother involved? Did Izzy's mother make a deal with Cambria to use necromancy to bring Izzy back and then use her as an assassin? Was she ever dead in the first place? These are only a few of the questions I have. The mystery is so convoluted; the truth buried so deed, I need help. I need..."

Sugarplums, I can't bring myself to say it.

"You need *me*."

His smugness makes me want to smack him.

"If the Queen is playing both sides of this game, we have our work cut out for us. Ditto if Izzy's mother is involved. We have to uncover their motives and find proof of what they're up to."

"So we start with our suspects. Cambria isn't talking, but she will."

"All I know is that my mother isn't telling me everything." I pause and hold his unflinching stare. "And neither are you."

He opens his hands wide, palms up. "What is it you wish to know?"

"Are you really planning on using your sister to take over this world?"

He chuckles. "No."

I scrutinize his features for any sign that he's lying. Of course, with a vampyre, you can't tell. "That's it?"

"You asked for the truth. I only wish to protect my sister. What happened to her is not her fault. It is mine."

"And the legends about her? Are they true?"

"A few."

That doesn't ease my mind. "But she's here, and...awake?"

He crosses the floor to me. "You are in no danger."

I want to believe him. "Who are you protecting her from now?"

"Any who seek to use her."

"Like other vampyres?"

A nod. "Those who have an unquenchable lust for power are always looking for a weapon. I must sabotage them, careful not to start a civil war, and never let them learn I am thwarting their attempts."

What a heavy weight to carry. What a risky game to play. "You're brave."

"Just so you know, she is not like a vampyre." He leans against the counter next to me. "She doesn't need blood or anything else to exist. She simply just does."

"Can she die?"

"I don't know. All things die, but she is…"

"What?" I have a feeling I'm not going to like the answer.

"The feather's magic was too much for her. Not only did it make her as immortal as an angel, it damaged her mind. She is but a child."

I think of Flower. "You mean mentally?"

"Yes."

These one-syllable responses are testing my patience, but the implications are far-reaching. "She's a child with incredible powers and an unstable mind. How in magic's name did you steal a feather from the Angel of Death?"

He strolls to the exit. "You'll have to ask Joseph about that. You might want to bring his favorite turnover when you do."

"Mayor Jo?" I remove my apron, tossing it on the table before following him. "Why?"

Torren stops and smiles at me. "Surely you can guess?"

My pulse speeds up, and I gape. "No way…"

"Fair night, Princess." He disappears, leaving me gawking.

"Wait! You can't drop that and leave!"

Mind whirling, I jump when he materializes in front of me again. "Yes, Mayor Jo is the Angel of Death, and yes, I'll be your partner. We make a good team." He winks. "Just like I knew we would."

My brain scrambles for a reply, but I trip over my tongue. "What? I... ah..."

"We'll begin our quest to solve these mysteries at after your Christmas gathering. Goodnight, Princess. Or should I say, *partner*?"

He offers a slight bow and vanishes.

Returning to the work table, I shake my head and laugh. What have I gotten myself into?

Epilogue

The three of us are up before dawn on Christmas morning, singing carols and baking. By the time the others begin arriving, the front of the shop is filled with garlands, pastries, and laughter.

Jo is the first to arrive, bringing us up to date on Chief Barnhill closing Betty's case. He's chalked it all up to a teenage prank gone wrong combined with an allergic reaction.

His wife and Betty's sister paid me a quick visit at my booth the previous day, letting me know they're aware there is more to the story and would like to lend their services to see that the true culprit is brought to justice. I assured them their assistance is appreciated, and I plan to ask one or both to aid me in uncovering what's happened to me and Izzy.

Mid-morning, all our guests are present. Cyn has brought a fresh tree for us to decorate, Maude has handed out toothbrush kits with bows, and Malena and Jo have snuck out back to exchange personal gifts.

Izzy and our ghost boy carry on random conversations, and

although I'm not surprised she sees him—ghost communication is a skill for those in the Black Heart Court—I am that she seems more comfortable with him than my friends.

Jo and Marlena come back inside, rubbing their hands to warm them. My godmother's cheeks are flushed and her smile is infectious. She makes cocoa for everyone.

Torren has brought Izzy a gift, which pleases me greatly. A collection of faery tales, a sketchbook, and a set of gel markers. Izzy is delighted, and after politely sipping her cocoa, she begs off and takes her stash upstairs.

"That was kind of you," I tell the vampyre.

"Art can be a mechanism for releasing the subconscious," he skims a finger down my arm. "It may help her remember what happened."

"Does your sister like to sketch?"

"Paint," he says. "And press flowers in books. I'm not sure that qualifies as art, but it makes her happy."

"I'd like to meet her."

His finger stills. "I would like you to."

I'm locked in his stare, his magic swirling around me like batter in a mixing bowl. "Would you like to step outside? I could use some fresh air."

His grin is wolfish. He entwines his fingers with mine. "That is the best present I think of."

Oh brother, Lady Wynnie complains as we pass her.

Unable to keep the smile off my face, I ignore her and lead Torren to a spot under the apple tree. Birds sing, and as we talk and laugh about inconsequential things—which feels good for a change—I catch faeries and goblin children peeking out from bushes and tree trunks to leave gifts for me.

Yes, this is my home for now, and I'm content to enjoy it.

* * *

Thank you for reading Candy and Creeps. Don't miss Seraphina's next adventure in Gumdrops and Ghouls, A Witchy Candy Shop Mystery, Book 3, coming in 2025!

Do you love cats, magic, and fun?

So do I!
That's why I created and love my Cozy Corner Reader
Community where my very special readers get exclusive short
stories from me, along with early access to all of my books.

I love to share recipes, pictures of my pets and plants, puzzles,
and coloring pages with my VIP readers!

A Cup of Catnip is only $5/month.
Furry Tales is $7/month and **includes my entire library** of
stories, including audiobooks.
https://reamstories.com/nyxhalliwell

I hope to see you there!

Visit My Store

Did you know you can buy directly from me? When you do, the retailer doesn't take a cut and I can pass on the savings to YOU!

https://www.nyxhalliwell.com/books

Benefits:
You can find ALL my books in one place
SAVE money
EARLY access to new releases
Special Collections and Limited Editions
Support a small business

Why Buy Direct?
When you purchase a book by your favorite author, electronic or print, on retailer platforms, the company keeps 30-70% of the sale, leaving the author with little to no profit (after the company deducts delivery fees, taxes, and other fees).

Buying directly from the author means that more goes to them so they can keep turning out stories for you. Every published story, every book, requires cover art, editing, and hours and hours of the author's time simply to create it. Not to mention overhead costs, such as websites, newsletters, writing software, graphics programs, advertising, taxes, etc.

In addition, one of the big-name retailers requires exclusivity, and all of them have terms of service and rules and regulations that make it challenging and time-consuming for an indie author to navigate the publishing world.

Most of us would MUCH rather spend our time creating more stories for YOU, rather than trying to jump through the hoops at the retailers. Buying direct from your favorite authors (where available) helps ensure that an author you love is not subject to unexplained account closures, withholding of royalties, censorship, and other issues that can affect their livelihood.

I've experienced ALL of these. By buying direct, you help put control of my work back in my hands - and I can continue to write more.

Either way, thank you for supporting me! I understand buying direct doesn't work for everyone and even if you use the retailers to buy my books, I appreciate you!

Happy reading,

Nyx

https://www.nyxhalliwell.com/books

Ready for more magick?

Don't miss the next exciting adventure! Sign up for Nyx's Cozy Clues Mystery Newsletter.

And check out these magical stories:

Sister Witches Of Raven Falls Mystery Series
Sister Witches of Raven Falls Special Collection
Of Potions and Portents
Of Curses and Charms
Of Stars and Spells
Of Spirits and Superstition
Sister Witches of Raven Falls Special Collection

Confessions of a Closet Medium Cozy Mystery Series
Confessions of a Closet Medium Special Collection
Pumpkins & Poltergeists
Magic & Mistletoe
Hearts & Haunts
Vows & Vengeance

Cupcakes & Corpses
Tea Leaves & Troubled Spirits
Haunted Honeymoon
Wedding Bells & Psychic Spells
Confessions of a Closet Medium Cozy Mystery Series

Sister Witches of Story Cove (Formerly Once Upon a Witch) Cozy Mystery Series

Cinder
Belle
Snow
Ruby
Zelle

Sister Witches of Story Cove Complete Set

Witchy Candy Shop Mysteries

Tricks and Treats
Candy and Creeps
Gum and Ghouls (releasing 2025)

Meet Nyx

USA Today bestselling author Nyx Halliwell loves writing magical stories as much as she loves baking and crafting. She believes cats really can talk (please don't tell her three rescue puppies), and yes, she sees ghosts.

She enjoys binge-watching mystery and paranormal shows with her hubby and reading all types of stories involving magic. She talks to trees, has too many crystals, and drinks far too much tea.

Check out her online store and sign up for her Cozy Corner newsletter at https://www.nyxhalliwell.com.

Dear Magical Reader

Thank you for reading this story! It is an honor and a privilege to write books for you. I'm an indie author and every fan is important to me. I pour my heart into each story and do my best to bring you a delightful escape from the real world.

Readers are the key to my success - not a traditional publishing deal (had four), an agent (had two), or a publicity team (yep, you guessed it, had several of those as well.)

Those of you who read my books and love my characters and worlds, and who then tell others, are like the best of friends. I adore you and will keep writing if you keep reading!

If you'd like to learn about my other books, sales, and special promotions, please sign up for my newsletter at https://www.nyxhalliwell.com.

Support me directly (no retailer taking their cut), grab special edition box sets, and get new releases before they are out at retailers by visiting my store https://www.nyxhalliwell.com/books. I have sales and offer NEW RELEASES early! Check it out.

Last but not least, if you enjoy grittier, but still fun, urban fantasy, paranormal romance, or romantic suspense, visit my pen name http://www.mistyevansbooks.com to see those books.

Thank you for supporting my dream.

Blessed be,

Nyx 🤍